HOUSEHOLD TALES

by the

BROTHERS GRIMM

illustrated by Mervyn Peake

with an introduction by Russell Hoban

PICADOR
published by Pan Books

The illustrations in this edition were first published 1946
by Eyre and Spottiswoode (Publishers) Ltd
Illustrations copyright 1948 under the Berne Convention
by Mervyn Peake
This edition first published 1973 by Methuen Children's Books Ltd
This Picador edition published 1977 by Pan Books Ltd,
Cavaye Place, London SW10 9PG
Text adaptation © Methuen Children's Books Ltd 1973
Illustrations © Maeve Peake 1973
Introduction © Russell Hoban 1977
ISBN 0 330 25036 1
Printed by Richard Clay (The Chaucer Press) Ltd, Bungay, Suffolk

Mervyn Peake was born in 1911 in Kuling, Central China, of medical missionary parents. He began to draw, paint and write stories at an early age, and his childhood environment exerted an influence on all his later work. He attended Tientsin Grammar School, and in England went to Eltham College and studied at the Royal Academy Schools. In the early 1930s, after a stay in Sark, he taught at the Westminster School of Art and started to exhibit his work. In 1937 he married Maeve Gilmore, then a sculpture student. They had three children.

He was called up in 1939, but in the army he managed to illustrate books, paint, write poetry and complete *Titus Groan*. Invalided out of the army, he worked at the Ministry of Information, and at the end of the war was sent to do drawings of devastated Europe, including the concentration camp at Belsen, much of which came into his later work in the form of poems and drawings and in *Titus Alone*. In 1946 he returned to Sark, later teaching at the Central School of Art and exhibiting his paintings in London, Europe and the United States.

His publications include the Gormenghast trilogy *(Titus Groan, Gormenghast* and *Titus Alone), A Book of Nonsense* and *Letters from a Lost Uncle,* and the poetry collections *Shapes and Sounds, The Glassblowers* and *The Rhyme of the Flying Bomb*. He died after a long illness in 1968.

By Mervyn Peake in Picador

Letters from a Lost Uncle
A Book of Nonsense

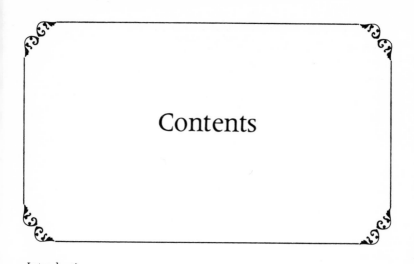

Contents

Introduction	7
The Three Sons of Fortune	21
The Nose-Tree	25
The Pack of Ragamuffins	33
The Seven Ravens	36
Old Sultan	39
The Mouse, the Bird and the Sausage	42
The Little Peasant	45
The Bremen Town-Musicians	52
Mother Hulda	57
The Elves: 1 and 2	62
Clever Grettel	66
King Thrushbeard	70
Our Lady's Child	76
Rumpelstiltskin	82
The Hut in the Forest	87
The Little Folks' Presents	93
Hans Married	96
The Twelve Huntsmen	98
Cat and Mouse in Partnership	102

The Golden Bird 106

The Rogue and His Master 115

The Wolf and the Seven Little Kids 118

Brother and Sister 124

The Turnip 131

Jorinda and Joringel 136

Hans in Luck 141

The Goose-Girl 147

The Three Feathers 154

The Poor Man and the Rich Man 158

The Peasant and the Devil 163

The Dog and the Sparrow 165

The Valiant Little Tailor 170

The Tom-Tit and the Bear 179

Giant Golden-Beard 184

The Three Spinners 191

The White Snake 195

The Poor Miller's Boy and the Cat 200

Briar Rose 205

The Singing, Soaring Lark 209

The Grave-Mound 216

One-Eye, Two-Eyes, and Three-Eyes 220

The Fox and the Horse 228

Master Pfriem 231

A Sad Story about a Snake 235

Snow-white and the Seven Dwarfs 237

The Wise Servant 246

Cinderella 248

Introduction

When I was a child it never occurred to me to wonder where these tales came from; they were simply there on the shelf waiting for me. Their first name was *Grimm's*, their middle name was *Fairy*, their last name was *Tales*, and that was that. Only in recent years have I come to know – I think it was my wife who told me – that Jacob Grimm (1785–1863) and Wilhelm Grimm (1786–1859) did not make up any of the stories; they went around collecting them from people who knew them by heart, had learnt them as a common resource passed from one generation to the next.

It's strange how a body of experience newly connected with a fact becomes new experience. Some of these tales I haven't read for years and years; many of them are altogether new to me. Now when I read them I feel the strands of story come into my mind as I might feel with my hands the weights and textures of ropes of pearls and ropes of sand, ropes of onions, thick hairy ropes of hemp, and fine silk threads and ribbons. Pearls and onions don't come out of nowhere.

I wasn't particularly looking for origins when I sat down to read these forty-seven tales so that I could write this introduction. I was simply pottering along quietly, making notes and waiting for something to happen. When something did happen it turned out to be the somewhere of a story's origin, revealing itself with startling swiftness and clarity and starting new thoughts in me.

It happened while I was reading *The Goose-Girl.* If you haven't read that story lately you should read it now before going on with this. I'll wait here.

My first notes after reading the story are:

Why had she no escort other than the maid-in-waiting? So that she'd be vulnerable? So the story could happen? Story is affecting out of proportion to events in it. Fall from high state to low one. False taken for true. Severed head. Speaking head. A gateway. A passage. An entrance and exit. A place for going in and out . . .

The head of the horse Falada in "the great dark-looking gateway" has made me feel the dark shapes moving in the darks of time, darks of earth. The idea of severed heads that talk is in us; when we meet it in a story there is no shock of surprise.

With dictionary in hand I go to the original German text. There the maid-in-waiting, the false bride, tells her husband to call the *Schinder,* the knacker, who will *"den Hals abhauen",* the neck cut off. In the English translation it's "cut off the head".

Curious about the use of *neck* instead of *head* in the original, I get the one-volume abridgement of *The Golden Bough** off the shelf to see what Frazer has to say about animal sacrifice. On p.618, after citing the ritual sacrifice of goats, oxen, and pigs, Frazer says:

. . . to put it generally, the corn-spirit is killed in animal form in autumn; part of his flesh is eaten as a sacrament by his worshippers; and part of it is kept till next sowing time or harvest as a pledge and security for the continuance or renewal of the corn-spirit's energies.

. . . in the cave of Phigalia in Arcadia the Black Demeter was portrayed with the head and mane of a horse on the body of a woman . . . The legend told of the Phigalian Demeter indicates that the horse was one of the animal forms assumed in ancient Greece, as in modern

* Macmillan Paperback 1957. (*The Golden Bough* was first published in twelve volumes in 1890; the abridgement was first published in 1922.)

Europe, by the corn-spirit. It was said that in her search for her daughter (Persephone) Demeter assumed the form of a mare to escape the addresses of Poseidon, and that, offended at his importunity, she withdrew in dudgeon to a cave not far from Phigalia in the highlands of Western Arcadia. There, robed in black, she tarried so long that the fruits of the earth were perishing, and mankind would have died of famine if Pan had not soothed the angry goddess and persuaded her to quit the cave. In memory of this event, the Phigalians set up an image of the Black Demeter in the cave; it represented a woman dressed in a long robe, with the head and mane of a horse. The Black Demeter, in whose absence the fruits of the earth perish, is plainly a mythical expression of the bare wintry earth stripped of its summer mantle of green.

Working back to p.603 I find:

Sometimes the corn-spirit appears in the shape of a horse or mare. Between Kalw and Stuttgart, when the corn bends before the wind, they say, "There runs the Horse". At Bohlingen, near Radolfzell in Baden, the last sheaf of oats is called the Oats-Stallion. In Hertfordshire, at the end of the reaping, there is, or used to be, observed a ceremony called "crying the Mare". The last blades of corn left standing on the field are tied together and called the Mare. The reapers stand at a distance and throw their sickles at it; he who cuts it through "has the prize, with acclamations and good cheer".

Elsewhere Frazer tells us that in Devon and Cornwall the last sheaf of the harvest is called "the neck"; *"nack"* in Devon dialect. That takes me back to the word *knacker. The Oxford English Dictionary* defines knacker as horse-slaughterer, and says that the origin of the word is obscure. It seems to me not at all unlikely that the word originally referred to the one who cut the horse's neck. In any case it was the German word for neck that put me on the track of Demeter and Persephone. Words have a way of doing that. Symbols change with time and place; the last sheaf of the harvest gathered many names, some of them echoed in *The Goose-Girl*: sometimes the last sheaf was "the gander's neck", sometimes it was "the bride". In some places a corn-puppet was ritually stripped as the princess in the tale was stripped of her finery by the maid-in-waiting; in other places the woman who bound the last sheaf was called "the Wheat-bride".

Back beyond the symbols stand other symbols; the names and sexes vary in a palimpsest of myth and history: back beyond Demeter and Persephone stand Isis and Osiris in Egyptian myth, Tammuz and Inanna in Sumerian. Beyond Dionysus torn in pieces at Thebes, beyond the body of Osiris dismembered we find the grim recall of human beings ritually slaughtered on the harvest-field. What is in us must be looked at.

Now consider the main elements of *The Goose-Girl*. Like Demeter and Persephone there are an old queen and her daughter, a *"Jungfer Königin"*, virgin queen. The princess is the true bride, the harvest bride promised to the prince. Between the old queen and the young queen there is a blood bond of communication, the little sacrifice of three drops of blood from the old queen's finger which is a little symbolic neck. The harvest bride goes *"weit über Feld"*, far over field. With her goes a maid-in-waiting, a season in waiting who strips the harvest bride and replaces her as the winter replaces the season of growth and harvest. The "false bride", the winter, has the neck of the horse/corn-spirit cut. Through the reign of winter, through the dark time of her reduction to a lower state, her comedown or descent, the true bride, who is both Demeter and Persephone, both harvest bride and young corn-spirit, talks to her Black Demeter corn-spirit mother, the head of Falada. Conrad the goose-boy plainly has designs on her. When the goose-girl, the ripening young virgin queen, undoes her golden hair, *"machte ihre Haare auf"*, opened her hair, Conrad would like to pluck a few of those hairs. He'd like to do some premature harvesting. But the promised bride-in-waiting calls on the wind to help her preserve her virginity. When her proper season comes, the true bride creeps into a stove, a womb-like place in which she reveals, like the Pythia at Delphi, the true state of things. The false bride, winter, is driven out and put to death, and the true bride, the young corn-spirit, reigns.

Characteristic of the myth-based tale is the absence of emotion where one would expect to find it. If we look at *The Goose-Girl* as story alone, we are left wondering about the maid-in-waiting, the "false bride" who

10

married the prince. Presumably they've slept together, lived together, had some kind of relationship. But the prince lets her be killed horribly, and apparently without a second thought, when the goose-girl is revealed as his true bride. Because this is not story-story: it is the transmission of mythic elements in story form; it is proto-story.

I don't speak German. My wife, however, is German and has done for me a literal translation of *The Goose-Girl*. Compare the very first words of the story:

Es lebte einmal eine alte Königin . . .

In this book you'll find that rendered:
Once upon a time there was a Queen . . .

Literally translated it is:
It lived once an old Queen . . .

"It lived once an old Queen . . ." Even that simple idiom is alive with the earthy awareness that something lives us. We are not an unconnected happening. The original language of these stories is better than any literary translation can hope to be – plain and powerful, quick with life and densely interwoven like an ancient hedge from which peep out the eyes of birds and mice. That steady ongoing voice that passes from one teller to the next resounds with earth and mortal echoes:

"O du Falada, da du hangest . . ."
"O du Jungfer Königin, da du gangest, . . ."

Do you hear the earth-feet, loam-feet, dancing slowly and the winds of season after season in that *"da du hangest"/"da du gangest"*? Here are blood and earth becoming word-music; here is the quickening of myth into art that lives its own life.

Granted that this folk tale is descended from a myth, why have I bothered to look for the myth in the folk tale, and why should you care whether it's there or not?

Consider fiction phenomenologically. The word itself is derived from the past participle of the Latin *fingere*, to shape, fashion, form or mould. We take it for granted that there will always be fiction of one kind or another in the form of stories: forming; shaping. Why do we take

11

that for granted? Why do we make fiction? Why do we say, "What if?"

We make fiction because we *are* fiction. Because there was a time when "it lived" us into being. Because there was a time when something said, "What if there are people?" A word, perhaps, whispered in the undulant amorphous ear of the primordial soup: "What if there are people, hey? What if?"

It lived us into being and it lives us still. We make stories because we are story. The fabric of our myths and folk tales is in us from before birth. The action systems of the universe are the origin of life and stories. The patterns of blue-green algae and the numinous wings of the Great Nebula in Orion and the runic scrawl of human chromosomes are stories. Begotten by no one knows what, stories beget people to live them. We are the offspring of immeasurable ideas.

The myths that are in us, whether they be of Demeter/Persephone's winter descent or Orpheus losing Eurydice, are the dynamics of thing-in-itself acting itself out in the collective being and consciousness of which each of us is a particle. When the goose-girl says:

> "Falada, Falada, hanging high . . ."

and the head answers:

> "Princess, Princess, passing by,
> Alas, alas! if thy mother knew it,
> Sadly, sadly, her heart would rue it."

we thrill to a mysterious sadness that is *familiar*. Even when we read the story for the first time, it seems not new to us but a recall of experience that is in us. An evocation rather than a recall, because the experience is not from a specific past but is always present in us *now*. As if we always have been and always are the true bride and the false one and the horse as well. As if all life and all experience are in all of us. It's as it is when we dream: the dreamer is all of the people in the dream; everybody and everything in the dream has been set in motion by the mind of . . . whom? Whose is the conscious and the dreaming mind? The physicist Erwin Schrödinger has said:*

* *What is Life?* AND *Mind and Matter*, Cambridge University Press, 1967.

... Mind is by its very nature a *singulare tantum*. I should say: the over-all number of minds is just one. I venture to call it indestructible since it has a peculiar time-table, namely mind is always *now*. There is really no before and after for mind. There is only a now that includes memories and expectations. But I grant that our language is not adequate to express this, and I also grant, should anyone wish to state it, that I am now talking religion, not science ...

It feels to me as if that's how it is: just one mind, and all of us know everything. Not intellectually but experientially. All of us have been, all of us are, everything. So if we ask the question: What is it to be us? and look for answers in our myths, we see being as a series of alternations. We have been, and we are, the true bride and the false one. "Falsely" rejected, we endure our season of darkness; "falsely" accepted, we enjoy the prince's bed and board; "rightfully" deposed, we die rolling naked in the nail-studded barrel; "rightfully" restored to our proper station, we thrive. We live our seasons as our seasons live us because that is the way of the universe: endless cycles of gain and loss, continual exchanges of energy.

No system is static; it is always in the process of becoming what it is not. Any putting-together charges whatever is put together with the energy that will tear it apart. The winding-down of one system is the winding-up of another. The condition is circular: it doesn't matter where you apparently enter the cycle. Be Eurydice lost, and the energy of that system will put together the Orpheus who has lost you and the music with which he will gain entrance to the nether world. Be Orpheus, and the energy of that system will be scattered when the Thracian women tear you apart. Be the Thracian women, and your tearing-apart of Orpheus will release the energy that puts him together again with Eurydice unlost. Eurydice and Orpheus and the Thracian women are only the costumes: the actors are the being lost, the losing and the finding, the gathering and the scattering. The actors are the action cycles continually moving in us and in all things.

If we are being lived by action cycles at the same time in us and beyond us, what is there for us to do? Everything. The action is abstractly *plus* or *minus*, *yang* or *yin*, *in* or *out*, *towards* or *away from*. It is we who clothe the action with ourselves. It is we who decide the character of the action, whether it be, in human terms, vital or deadly.

Around us all is night, black night that howls outside the circle of our words or crouches magically with the fire reflected in its eyes. We are in it; it is in us. We need to know that night and we need not to know. Our primal "What if?" is the twining of our fingers in the dark with those of unseen Chance and whispering Dread who walk with us. They are sister and brother to us, father and mother: the ancient family of not-knowing, walking in uncertainty.

In that uncertainty our stories go with us on roads of luck and death, of love and lostness. Burn all the books, and still there will be stories. Make a law requiring forty hours of television-watching weekly, and still there will be stories. Charred by fire or burnt out by electronics, stories will put themselves together out of ashes and broken glass and melted wire; and not perhaps such stories as we might like. But they will live us according to their need because we are a fiction, a continual forming and shaping.

That's why it matters that the myths be found and recognized in old and smooth-rubbed stories: to make a fire in the night and a clear space in the silence where the voice of all our past and immanent *now* can sound; to keep us from losing the story of us. We are not a random happening: the seasons of the earth are in us, and the seasons of the galaxies, the tides of the expanding universe as well. We are the true bride and the false one acting out a cycle not of our invention. Perhaps there still is time for us to find a way of doing it with hands shaped to the things of life, with death a natural exchange of rounded strophes rather than a monster madness gabbling in the dark.

That's why Grimm is worth a closer look. These are household tales for a world that is one single household. In these stories we can find our way not back, but forward to the story of us.

You will remember that it was the idea of the horse's head in the gateway that made me wonder about the origins of *The Goose-Girl*. It isn't at all surprising that horses figure in so many different ways in myth and story – there is such power in them beyond the physical. The prehistoric life in them seems whole and intact. Any horse you meet seems to have in it a knowing that is deeper, older, more primal than our own; they seem witnesses to something lost to the sight of human-kind. There is something important about horses. See a great dark cart-horse in the rain, steam coming up from its back; go out to a stable in the cold dark of a winter morning: when horses look at you, where they look from is not where we look from. I believe that most of us would like to be thought well of by horses.

Before the motorcar replaced the horse, and for some years after, there were many illustrators who drew horses with the same authority with which they drew the human figure; now there are very few who can do that. Most modern illustrators fudge a horse the best they can and hope to get by on technique. Mervyn Peake's horses are of a piece with his people: some are knaves, some are drudges, and some of them are magical.

The drawing of the goose-girl talking to the head of Falada is a picture that one can look at for a long time. The horse is one of Peake's magical beasts. The great dead eyes are certainly not horse's eyes, they are *other*. They make one think of a deer but also of a praying mantis. They are disquieting, disturbing, disorienting: if a horse has eyes like that, then anything might be almost anything, and gone are the guarantees implicit in the ordinary look of things.

The head of Falada is not realistically nailed to the wall; the neck and head simply grow out of the wall that divides a world of shadow from a world of light. The dense hatching of the shadow side of the wall seems the particulate face of time itself. Through the archway stream the white geese into the light on the distant meadows and hills.

The figure of the goose-girl is as conventional and delicate as a Dresden shepherdess, not only the look but the gesture – one almost expects her to be standing on a round china base rather than on the ground. The shadow-particles of time dance about her as she looks up at the other-real speaking head of Falada, and the bright and ordinary prettiness of the girl becomes eerie and astonishing: that great shadowy wall is so high, the head of the horse is so powerful in its otherness – how can the girl endure the forces flickering through and around her! For she obviously does endure them, she becomes powerful enough magically and graphic-ally to balance the array of weights and forces. Because each look at the girl is a fresh realization of that action, the simple composition is kept moving. The effect is heightened if you place the book to one side rather than directly in front of you and let your eyes go out of focus: as your vision shifts in and out of its normal binocular function, the arch of light in the opening of the wall moves back towards the goose-girl and away, back and away; the goose-girl moves into and out of the arch of light, and the geese hurry towards the meadows.

And still that horse's head will not let go of me. I go to the Goethe Institut Library in Princes Gate. There our friends Hanna Tormouche and Luise von Loew bring down thick books from the shelves for me, such treasures as the *Handwörterbuch des Deutschen Aberglaubens (Dictionary of German Superstitions)*. There I find all kinds of things, the words themselves seem to have the shape and timbre of the ideas in them, as: *das Pferd als Führer des Toten*, the horse as guide of the dead. Long and bony and hoof-clopping, those words.

Horses' heads were hung on trees at the shrine of Odin in Uppsala. Horses' heads on poles and fences were used to avert evil. Horses' heads were put on ridgepoles and the gable ends of houses (in Celle in Lower Saxony, where my wife was born, you can still see the barge-boards at the gable ends carried up to crossed horses' heads at the ridge of the roof). Horses' heads in so many times and places! Horses' heads buried under doorsteps; last-sheaf horses' heads; the cut-off head of the "October Horse" decorated with loaves of bread. And coming back from the Goethe Institut I pass, on the Fulham Road in London just a few doors from where this book is published, a horse's head over a gateway at the Hungry Horse Restaurant.

These things whirl in my head, and I find that whirling gyroscopically stabilizing. Society relegates to superstition that range of signification that it cannot use in the reality-frame of every day, but reality does not end at the limits of society's frail consensus; the unknowable thingness of things and the ideas that emanate from it are equally real with all things else. Myth and story have the practical function of keeping us in touch with the unknown and unknowable in ourselves and in the universe. The more awareness we have of the other-than-rational in us, the better able we are to be reasonable in our actions.

Goya wrote – I think it was on the title-page of *Los Caprichos* – "The dream of Reason produces monsters". I don't think that's how it is.

16

I think it's when reason is *not* allowed to dream that it acts out its dreams while awake, and then it is that monsters are produced, in Goya's time and in ours. Modern scientists studying the phenomena of sleep have found that the person who is prevented from dreaming soon cannot function properly when awake. I believe that both as individuals and as a society we can find a healthy balance only when our minds (or mind) can move freely from the ordinary to the extraordinary reality-frame. The healthy mind knows where it is and draws its sustenance from different realms for dream and waking action. The danger of those fictions current now in television, films, and government is that violent and uncontrollable dreams have moved out of the realm of the extra-ordinary and into the ordinary, there to become part of our stock of usable action. Our rapists and our hooligans and our armament-racing heads of state are wide awake and going about their ordinary business.

Enough of that. *The Goose-Girl* has taken me *weit über Feld*. With that one tale my tracing of origins and my metaphysical speculations begin and end. *Household Tales* will happen to you according to how you are and where you are when you read them. With or without detective-work these stories will put you someplace you have never been before; that action is ongoing in them and in you. The best of it is, I think, the tingling of not-knowing and knowing at the same time. Be the youngest simple son or daughter, go into the world and take your chance. Encounter, in a state of not-knowing, whatever comes your way: three wishes, three giants or three labours. Find supernatural helpers, little people, speaking animals or devils; make magical descents to depths where toads give golden rings and talismans. And all the time feel in you the knowing that *if* the trapdoor opens, *if* the helper beckons, *if* the chance should offer, it will not be missed.

At the Goethe Institut Library I borrowed Ruth Michaelis-Jena's *The Brothers Grimm**. If this essay should introduce you to that book as well as this one, my time will have been well spent.

The mother of Jacob and Wilhelm Grimm was born Dorothea Zimmer; their father was Philipp Wilhelm Grimm, town clerk at Hanau. In 1791 he became *Amtmann* (justiciary) of Steinau, a little town in the Kinzig valley. There were five children then, all boys: Jacob was

* Routledge & Kegan Paul, 1970.

six years old; Wilhelm five; Carl four; Ferdinand three; and Ludwig one. A sister, Charlotte Amalie, was born in 1793.

Ruth Michaelis-Jena tells us:

> ... The *Amtshaus* ... was a handsome half-timbered building, surrounded by gardens and a walled courtyard. The façade had consoles and rafters, finely carved with scrolls and fantastic figures. One irregular beam ended in a little squinting devil which both fascinated and frightened the children. There were stables and outhouses, a turret stair and a huge lime tree at the front door.

If one were to design the perfect childhood, it would be such a one as the brothers Grimm enjoyed in Steinau: they had a loving, cheerful mother and a good father who wore "a blue frock coat, with red velvet collar and gold epaulettes, leather breeches and boots with silver spurs"; there were postilions and horses, foresters and goose-girls; woods and hills and fields; storks and swallows, cows and sheep; festivals and traditions; sowing and reaping and spinning in the natural order of the seasons.

The idyll ended with the death of their father in 1796 but the goodness of that childhood lasted. From the time they first saw the light of day, Jacob and Wilhelm Grimm had found themselves in an abundant world and among people who cared for one another in a network of love and attention and practical detail. No misfortune or later unhappiness could stand up against that. All their lives they remained true and loving to each other and the people and the world around them. They lived in a constant opening up of sense and intellect, a continual deepening of fidelity that animated for them voices scarcely heard and half-forgotten – earth voices whose words and timbre they would labour to preserve. "The very blood can call and speak . . ." they said, and they listened.

The brothers Grimm knew well what they were doing, knew the myths that lay behind them, knew these tales' proper place in social and in literary evolution. They worked not for some prettified ideal of childhood but for the ongoing "What if?" that is humankind. What they did in their work with language and folklore was simply to repay with everything that was in them the life that gave them life and the world that gave them world. With loving care and steadfast labour they gathered and they gleaned as if they themselves were one double avatar of the fruitful corn-spirit, offering with full hands their plenty to us then and now and later.

In the introduction to the first edition of *Household Tales,* published in 1812, Jacob and Wilhelm Grimm wrote:

... when the heavens have unleashed a storm, or when some other natural disaster has battered down a whole harvest, we may well find that in some sheltered corner by the roadside, under hedges and shrubs, a few ears of corn have survived. When the sun begins to shine again, they will grow, hidden and unnoticed. No early scythe will cut them for the corn-houses. Only late in summer, when the ears are ripe and heavy with grain, some poor humble hand will glean them, and bind them carefully, one by one. The little bundles will be carried home, more cherished than big sheaves, and will provide food for the winter, and perhaps the only seed for the future ...

RUSSELL HOBAN, London, 17 October, 1976

The Three Sons
of Fortune

A father called his three sons to him, and gave the first a cock, the second a scythe, and the third a cat.

"I am old," said he. "I shall not live long, and I wish to provide for you before my end; money I have not, and what I now give you seems of little worth, but all depends on your making a sensible use of it. Just seek out a country where such things are still unknown, and your fortune is made."

After the father's death the eldest son went away with his cock, but wherever he came cocks were already known; in towns he saw them from a distance, sitting upon steeples and turning round with the wind, and in villages he heard more than one crowing. No one showed any wonder at the creature, so that it did not look as if he would make his fortune by it. At last, however, he came to an island where the people knew nothing about cocks, and did not even understand how to tell the time. They knew when it was morning or evening, but at night not one of them knew how to find out the hour.

"Look," said the eldest son, "what a proud creature this cock is! It has a ruby-red crown upon its head, and wears spurs like a knight; it calls you three times during the night, at fixed hours, and when it calls for the last time, the sun soon rises. But if it crows in broad daylight, then take notice, for there will certainly be a change of weather."

The people were well pleased; for a whole night they did not sleep, and listened with great delight as the cock at two, four, and six o'clock loudly and clearly proclaimed the time. They asked if the cock were for sale, and how much he wanted for it.

"About as much gold as an ass can carry," answered he.

"A ridiculously small price for such a precious creature!" they cried unanimously, and willingly gave him what he had asked.

When he came home with his wealth his brothers were astonished, and the second said, "Well, I'll set out and see whether I can get rid of my scythe as profitably." But it did not look as if he would, for labourers met him everywhere, and all had scythes upon their shoulders.

At last, however, he came to an island where the people knew nothing of scythes. When the corn was ripe there, they took cannon out to the fields and shot it down. Now this was rather a chancy business: many shot right over it, others hit the ears instead of the stems and shot them away, so that much corn was lost – and besides, it made a terrible noise. So the man set to work and mowed it down so quietly and quickly that the people gaped in astonishment. They agreed to give him what he wanted for the scythe, and he received a horse laden with as much gold as it could carry.

And now the third brother wanted to try his luck with his cat. He fared just like the others: so long as he stayed on the mainland there was nothing to be done. Every place had cats – so many of them that new-born kittens were generally drowned in the ponds.

At last he sailed over to an island, and as luck would have it no cats had ever been seen there, and the mice had got the upper hand so much that they danced upon the tables and benches whether the masters were at home or not. The people complained bitterly of the plague of mice. The King himself in his palace was not safe from them: mice squeaked in every corner, and gnawed whatever they could lay hold of. But now the cat began to catch them, and the people begged the King to buy this wonderful animal. The King willingly gave what was asked, which was a mule laden with gold, and the third brother came home with the greatest treasure of all.

The cat made merry with the mice in the royal palace, and killed so many that they could not be counted. At last she grew thirsty, so she lifted up her head and cried, "Mew! Mew!" When they heard this strange cry, the King and all his people were frightened, and in their terror ran helter skelter out of the palace. Then the King took counsel what was best to be done. At last it was determined to send a herald to the cat, and demand that she should leave the palace. If not, force would be used against her.

The councillors said, "We would rather be plagued with the mice, for to that misfortune we are accustomed, than give up our lives to such a monster as this." A noble youth, therefore, was sent to ask the cat whether she would peaceably quit the castle. But the cat, whose thirst had become still greater, merely answered, "Mew! mew!" The youth understood her to say, "Most certainly not! Most certainly not!" and took this answer to the King.

"Then," said the councillors, "she shall yield to force."

Cannon were brought out, and the palace was soon in flames. When the fire reached the room where the cat was sitting, she sprang safely out of the window; but the besiegers did not leave off until the whole palace was shot to the ground.

The Nose-tree

Did you ever hear the story of the three poor soldiers, who, after having fought hard in the wars, set out on their road home, begging their way as they went?

They had journeyed a long way, sick at heart with their bad luck at thus being turned loose on the world, and they no longer young, when one evening they reached a gloomy wood, through which lay their road. Night came fast upon them, and they found that they must, however unwillingly, sleep in this wood; so it was agreed that two should lie down and sleep, while a third sat up and watched, lest wild beasts should tear them to pieces. When he was tired he was to wake the second and sleep in his turn; and so on with the last, so as to share the work fairly among them.

The two who were to rest first soon lay down and fell fast asleep; and the other made himself a good fire under the trees, and sat down by its side to keep watch. He had not sat long before up came a dwarf in a red jacket.

"Who is there?" said he.

"A friend," said the soldier.

"What sort of a friend?"

"An old broken soldier," said the other, "with his two comrades, who have nothing left to live on. Come, sit down and warm yourself."

"Well, my worthy fellow," said the little man, "I will do what I can for you; take this and show it to your comrades in the morning." So he took out an old cloak and gave it to the soldier, telling him that whenever he put it over his shoulders anything that he wished for would be done for him. Then the little man made a bow and walked away.

The second soldier's turn to watch soon came. He had not sat long by himself before up came the dwarf in the red jacket again. The soldier treated him in as friendly a way as his comrade had done, and the little man gave him a purse, which he told him would always be full of gold, however much he drew out of it.

Then the third soldier's turn to watch came; and he also had little Red-jacket for his guest, who gave him a wonderful horn, that drew crowds round it whenever it was played, and made everyone forget his business to come and dance to its beautiful music.

In the morning each told his story, and showed the gift he had got from the elf; and as they all liked each other very much, and were old friends, they agreed to travel together to see the world, and, for a while, only to make use of the wonderful purse. And thus they spent their time very joyously, till at last they began to be tired of this roving life, and thought they would like to have a home of their own. So the first soldier put his old cloak on, and wished for a fine castle. In a moment it stood before their eyes: fine gardens and green lawns spread round it, and flocks of sheep, and goats, and herds of oxen were grazing about; and out of the gate came a grand coach with three dapple-grey horses, to meet them and bring them home.

All this was very well for a time, but they found it would not do to stay at home always; so they got together all their rich clothes, and jewels, and money, and ordered their coach with three dapple-grey horses, and set out on a journey to see a neighbouring king. Now this king had an only daughter, and as he saw the three soldiers travelling in such grand style, he took them for king's sons, and so gave them a kind welcome.

One day, as the second soldier was walking with the princess, she saw that he had the wonderful purse in his hand. She asked him what it was, and he was foolish enough to tell her – though, indeed, it did not much signify what he said, for she was a fairy, and knew all the wonderful things that the three soldiers brought. Now this princess was very cunning and artful; so she set to work and made a purse, so like the soldier's that no one would know one from the other; and then she asked him to come and see her, and made him drink some wine that she had got ready for him, and which soon made him fall fast asleep. Then she felt in his pocket, and took away the wonderful purse, and left the one she had made in its place.

The next morning the soldiers set out for home; and soon after they had reached their castle, happening to want some money, they went to their purse for it, and found some in it; but to their great sorrow, when they had emptied it, no money came in the place of what they took. Then the deception was soon found out; for the second soldier remembered that he had told the story to the princess, and he guessed that she had played him a trick.

"Alas!" cried he. "Poor wretches that we are, what shall we do?"

"Oh!" said the first soldier. "Let no grey hairs grow for this mishap. I'll soon get the purse back." So he threw his cloak across his shoulders and wished himself in the princess's chamber.

There he found her sitting alone, counting her gold, that fell around her in a shower from the wonderful purse.

But the soldier stood looking at her too long; she turned, saw him, and cried out, "Thieves! Thieves!" so that the whole court came running in, and tried to seize him. The poor soldier was dreadfully frightened, and thought it was high time to escape. So, without thinking of the ready way of travelling that his cloak gave him, he ran to the window, opened it, and jumped out. Unluckily, in his haste, his cloak caught and was left hanging, to the great joy of the princess, who knew its worth.

The poor soldier made the best of his way home to his comrades on foot, and in a very downcast mood; but the third soldier told him to take heart, and took his horn and blew a merry tune. At the first blast countless men on foot and horseback came rushing to their aid, and they set out to make war against their enemy. Then the king's palace was besieged, and he was told that he must give up the purse and cloak, or not one stone would be left upon another. And the king went into his daughter's chamber and talked with her; but she said, "Let me try first if I cannot beat them in some way or another."

So she thought of a cunning scheme to outwit them; and dressing herself as a poor girl, with a basket on her arm, she set out by night with her maid and went into the enemy's camp, as if she wanted to sell trinkets.

In the morning she began to ramble about, singing ballads so beautifully that all the tents were left empty, and the soldiers hurried up in crowds, and thought of nothing but hearing her sing. Among the rest came the soldier to whom the horn belonged, and as soon as she saw him she winked to her maid, who slipped slyly through the crowd, and went into his tent where it hung, and stole it. This done they both got safely back to the palace, the besieging army went away, the three wonderful gifts were all left in the hands of the princess, and the three soldiers were as penniless and forlorn as when little Red-jacket found them in the wood.

Poor fellows! They began to think what to do now.

"Comrades," at last said the second soldier, who had had the purse, "we had better part; we cannot live together; let each seek his bread as well as he can." So he turned to the right, and the other two went to the left, for they said they would rather travel together. Then on the second soldier wandered till he came to a wood (the same wood where they had met with so much good luck before), and when evening began to fall, he sat down tired beneath a tree, and soon fell asleep.

Morning dawned, and he was delighted, on opening his eyes, to see that the tree was laden with the most beautiful apples. He was hungry, so he soon plucked and ate first one, then a second, then a third apple. A strange feeling came over his nose; when he put the apple to his mouth something was in the way. He felt it – it was his nose, that grew and grew till it hung down to his breast. It did not stop there – still it grew and grew.

"Heavens!" thought he. "When will it have done growing?" And well might he ask, for by this time it reached the ground as he sat on the grass, and it kept creeping on, till he could not bear its weight or raise himself up; and it seemed as if it would never end, for already it stretched its enormous length all through the wood, over hill and dale.

Meanwhile his comrades were journeying on, till on a sudden one of them stumbled against something.

"What can that be?" said the other. They looked, and could think of nothing that it was like but a nose.

"We will follow it and find its owner," said they. So they traced it back, till at last they found their poor comrade, lying under the apple-tree.

What was to be done? They tried to carry him, but in vain. They caught an ass that was passing, and raised him upon its back; but it soon tired of carrying such a load. So they sat down in despair. Before long up came their old friend the dwarf with the red jacket.

"Why, how now, friend?" said he, laughing. "Well, I must find a cure for you, that's certain." So he told them to gather a pear from another tree that grew close by, and the nose would come right again. No time was lost; and the nose was soon brought to its proper size, to the poor soldier's joy.

"I will do something more for you," said the dwarf. "Take some of those pears and apples with you. Whoever eats one of the apples will have his nose grow like yours just now; but if you give him a pear, all will come right again. Go to the princess, and get her to eat some of your apples; her nose will grow twenty times as long as yours did. Then use your wits, and you will get what you want from her."

They thanked their old friend heartily for all his kindness; and it was agreed that the poor soldier, who had already tried the power of the apple, should undertake the task. So he dressed himself up as a gardener's boy, and went to the king's palace, and said he had apples to sell, so fine and so beautiful as were never seen before. Everyone that saw them was delighted, and wanted to taste; but he said they were only for the princess; and she soon sent her maid to buy his stock. They were so ripe and rosy that she began eating; and she had not eaten above a dozen before she too began to wonder what ailed her nose, for it grew and grew down to the ground, out at the window, and over the garden and away, nobody knew where.

Then the king made known to all his kingdom that whoever would heal her of this dreadful disease should be richly rewarded. Many tried, but the princess got no relief. And now the old soldier dressed himself up very sprucely as a doctor, and said he would cure her. So he chopped up some of the apple, and, to punish her a little more, gave her a dose, saying he would call tomorrow and see her again. The morrow came, and of course instead of being better the nose had been growing on all night as before; and the poor princess was in a dreadful fright. So the doctor chopped up a very little of the pear and gave it to her, and said he would call again the next day. Next day came, and the nose was a little smaller, but yet it was bigger than when the doctor first began to meddle with it.

Then he thought to himself, "I must frighten this cunning princess a little more before I shall get what I want from her." So he gave her another dose of the apple, and said he would call on the morrow. The morrow came, and the nose was ten times as bad as before.

"My good lady," said the doctor, "something works against my medicine, and is too strong for it; but I know by the force of my art what it is: you have stolen goods about you, I am sure; and if you do not give them back, I can do nothing for you."

The princess denied very stoutly that she had anything of the kind.

"Very well," said the doctor, "you may do as you please, but I am sure I am right, and you will die if you do not admit it." Then he went to the king, and told him how the matter stood.

"Daughter," said the king, "send back the cloak, the purse, and the horn that you stole from the rightful owners."

Then she ordered her maid to fetch all three, and gave them to the doctor, and begged him to give them back to the soldiers; and the

moment he had them safe he gave her a whole pear to eat, and the nose came right. Then he put on the cloak, wished the king and all his court a good day, and was soon with his two friends, who lived from that time happily at home in their palace, except when they took an airing to see the world, in their coach with the three dapple-grey horses.

The Pack
of Ragamuffins

The cock once said to the hen, "The nuts are ripe, so let us go to the hill together and eat our fill before the squirrel gets them all."

They went to the hill, and as it was a bright day they stayed till evening. Now whether it was that they had eaten till they were too fat, or whether they had become proud, at any rate they refused to go home on foot, and the cock had to build a little carriage of nut-shells. When it was ready, the little hen seated herself in it and said to the cock, "Now you can harness yourself to it."

"I like that!" said the cock. "I'd rather go home on foot than let myself be harnessed to it; no, that's not our bargain. I don't mind being coachman and sitting on the box, but drag it myself I will not."

As they were thus disputing, a duck quacked to them, "You thieving folks, who bade you steal the nuts? You shall suffer for it!" and ran with open beak at the cock. But the cock boldly attacked the duck, and at last wounded her so with his spurs that she begged for mercy, and willingly let herself be harnessed to the carriage as a punishment. The little cock sat on the box and was coachman, and they went off at a gallop, the cock shouting, "Duck, go as fast as you can."

When they had driven a part of the way they met two foot-passengers, a pin and a needle, who cried "Stop! stop!" and said that they could not go a step further, as it was so dirty on the road. They

33

asked if they could get into the carriage for a while. As they were thin people, who did not take up much room, the cock let them both get in, but they had to promise him and his little hen not to step on their feet.

Late in the evening they came to an inn, and as they did not like to go further by night, they went in. The host at first made many objections: his house was already full, besides he thought they could not be very distinguished persons; but at last, as they made pleasant speeches, and told him that he could have the egg which the little hen had laid on the way, and could likewise keep the duck, which laid one every day, he at length said that they might stay the night. And now they were well served, and feasted and made merry.

Early in the morning, when day was breaking, and everyone was asleep, the cock awoke the hen, brought the egg, pecked it open, and they ate it together, but they threw the shell on the hearth. The duck, who liked to sleep in the open air and had stayed in the yard, was merry as a lark when she heard them going away. She found a stream, down which she swam, which was a much quicker way of travelling than being harnessed to a carriage. The host did not get out of bed for two hours after this; he washed himself and dried himself with his towel. The pin in it made a red scratch from one ear to the other. After this he went into the kitchen and wanted to light a pipe, but when he bent over the hearth the egg-shell darted into his eyes.

"This morning everything attacks my head," said he, and angrily sat down on his grandfather's chair, but he quickly started up again and cried, "Woe is me," for the needle had pricked him still worse than the pin, and not in the head. Now he was thoroughly angry, and suspected the guests who had come so late the night before. When he looked for them, they were gone. Then he made a vow to take no more raga-muffins into his house, for they consume much, pay for nothing, and play mischievous tricks into the bargain by way of gratitude.

The Seven Ravens

There was once a man who had seven sons, and still he had no daughter, however much he wished for one. At length his wife again gave him hope of a child, and when it came into the world it was a girl. Their joy was great, but the child was sickly and small, and had to be privately baptized on account of its weakness. The father sent one of the boys in haste to the spring to fetch water for the baptism. The other six went with him, and as each of them wanted to be first to fill it, the jug fell into the well. There they stood, not knowing what to do, for none of them dared to go home. When they did not return, the father grew impatient, and said, "Those wicked boys have forgotten the water, playing some game!" He was afraid the girl would die without being baptized, and in his anger cried, "I wish the boys were all turned into ravens."

Hardly was the word spoken before he heard a whirring of wings over his head, looked up and saw seven coal-black ravens flying away. The parents could not reverse the curse, and however sad they were at the loss of their seven sons, they comforted themselves with their dear little daughter, who soon grew strong and every day became more beautiful. For a long time she did not know that she had had brothers, for her parents were careful not to mention them when she was near, but one day she accidentally heard some people saying of herself, that she was certainly beautiful, but that in reality she was to blame for the misfortune which had befallen her seven brothers. Then she was much troubled, and went to her father and mother and asked if it was true that she had brothers, and what had become of them.

The parents told her that what had befallen her brothers was the will of Heaven, and that her birth had only been the innocent cause. But every day the maiden grieved, and she had no rest or peace until she set out secretly into the wide world to trace her brothers and set them free, whatever the cost. She took nothing with her but a little ring belonging to her parents, as a keepsake, a loaf of bread against hunger, a little pitcher of water against thirst, and a little chair against weariness.

And now she went continually onwards, far, far, to the very end of the world. Then she came to the sun, but it was too hot and terrible and burned little children. Hastily she ran away, and ran to the moon, but it was far too cold and malicious, and when it saw the child, it said, "I smell, I smell the flesh of men." At this she ran swiftly away, and came to the stars, which were kind and good to her. Each of them sat on its own particular little chair. But the morning star arose, and gave her the leg bone of a chicken, and said, "Without this drumstick you cannot open the Glass Mountain, and in the Glass Mountain are your brothers."

The maiden took the drumstick, wrapped it carefully in a cloth, and went onwards again until she came to the Glass Mountain. The door was shut, and she decided to take out the drumstick; but when she undid the cloth, it was empty, and she had lost the good star's present. What was she to do now? How could she rescue her brothers, with no key to the Glass Mountain? The good sister took a knife, cut off one of her little fingers, put it in the door, and succeeded in opening it. Inside, a little dwarf came to meet her, who said, "My child, what are you looking for?"

"I am looking for my brothers, the seven ravens," she replied.

The dwarf said, "The lord ravens are not at home, but if you will wait here until they come, step in."

Thereupon the little dwarf carried the ravens' dinner in, on seven little plates and in seven little glasses, and the sister ate a morsel from

37

each plate, and from each little glass she took a sip, but in the last little glass she dropped the ring which she had brought with her.

Suddenly she heard a whirring of wings and a rushing through the air, and the little dwarf said, "Now the lord ravens are flying home." They came, wanted to eat and drink, and looked for their little plates and glasses. Then said one after the other, "Who has eaten something from my plate? Who has drunk out of my little glass? It was a human mouth." And when the seventh came to the bottom of the glass, the ring rolled against his mouth. When he saw that it was a ring belonging to his father and mother, he said, "God grant that our sister be here, and then we shall be free."

When the maiden, who was standing behind the door watching, heard that wish, she came out, and at once all the ravens were restored to their human form again. And they embraced and kissed each other, and went joyfully home.

Old Sultan

A farmer once had a faithful dog called Sultan, who had grown old, and lost all his teeth, so that he could no longer hold anything fast. One day the farmer was standing with his wife before the house-door, and said, "Tomorrow I intend to shoot Old Sultan; he is no longer of any use."

His wife, who felt pity for the faithful beast, answered, "He has served us so long, and been so faithful, that we might well give him his keep."

"What?" said the man. "That's a stupid thing to say. He hasn't a tooth left in his mouth, and no thief is afraid of him. Let's get rid of him. If he has served us well, he has been well fed in return."

The poor dog, who was lying stretched out in the sun not far off, had heard everything, and was sorry that the morrow was to be his last day. He had a good friend, the wolf, and he crept out in the evening into the forest to him, and bemoaned his fate.

"Cheer up, my friend," said the wolf. "I will help you out of your trouble. Tomorrow, early in the morning, your master is going with his wife to make hay, and they'll take their child with them. No one will be left in the house. During work-time they usually lay the child under the hedge in the shade; you lay yourself there too, just as if you wished to guard it. Then I will come out of the wood, and carry off the child. You must rush swiftly after me as if to rescue it from me. I will let it

39

fall, and you will take it back to its parents who will think that you have saved it, and will be so grateful that they will never let you want for anything again."

The plan was carried out just as it was arranged. The father screamed when he saw the wolf running across the field with his child, but when Old Sultan brought it back he was full of joy, and stroked him and said, "Not a hair of yours shall be hurt; you shall eat my bread free as long as you live." And to his wife he said, "Go home at once and make Old Sultan some bread and milk that he will not have to bite, and bring the pillow out of my bed. I will give him that to lie on."

Henceforward Old Sultan was as well off as he could wish to be.

Soon afterwards the wolf visited him, and was pleased that everything had succeeded so well. "But, friend," said he, "I hope you'll just look the other way if, when I have a chance, I carry off one of your master's fat sheep."

"Do not count on that," answered the dog. "I will remain true to my master; I cannot agree to that."

The wolf, who thought that this could not be spoken in earnest, came slinking round the farm in the night to steal a sheep. But the farmer, to whom the faithful Sultan had told the wolf's plan, caught him and whacked his hide soundly with the flail. The wolf was sent packing,

40

but he cried to the dog, "Just you wait, you scoundrel, you shall pay for this."

The next morning the wolf sent the boar to challenge the dog to come out into the forest so that they might settle the affair. Old Sultan could find no one to stand by him but a cat with only three legs, and as they went out together the poor cat limped along, her tail stretched out with pain.

The wolf and his friend were already on the spot appointed, but when they saw their enemy coming they thought that he was bringing a sword with him, for they mistook the outstretched tail of the cat for one. And when the poor beast hopped on its three legs, they could only think every time that it was picking up a stone to throw at them. So they were both afraid; the wild boar crept into the undergrowth and the wolf jumped up a tree.

When the dog and the cat came up, they were surprised to find no one there. The wild boar, however, had not been able to hide himself altogether; and one of his ears could still be seen. While the cat was looking carefully about, the boar moved his ear; the cat thought it was a mouse, jumped upon it and bit it hard. The boar made a fearful noise and ran away, crying out, "The guilty one is up in the tree." The dog and cat looked up and saw the wolf, who was ashamed of being such a coward and made friends with the dog again.

The Mouse,
the Bird, and the Sausage

Once on a time a mouse, a bird, and a sausage became companions, kept house together, lived well and happily with each other, and wonderfully increased their possessions. The bird's work was to fly every day into the forest and bring back wood. The mouse had to carry water, light the fire, and lay the table, but the sausage had to cook.

He who is too well off is always longing for something new. One day the bird met another bird, to whom it related its excellent circumstances and boasted of them. The other bird, however, called it a poor simpleton for its hard work, and said that the two at home had an easy life. For when the mouse had made her fire and carried her water, she went into her little room to rest until she had to lay the cloth. The sausage stayed by the pot, saw that the food was cooking well, and, when it was nearly time for dinner, it rolled itself once or twice through the broth and vegetables, and that was all it had to do to make them buttered, salted, and ready. When the bird came home with his burden of wood, they sat down to dinner. After they had had their meal, they slept their fill till next morning – a fine life for the mouse and the sausage!

Next day the bird, prompted by the other bird, would go no more into the wood, saying that he had been servant long enough, and had been made a fool of by the mouse and the sausage, and that they must do the work in turn. The mouse and the sausage argued about it, but

the bird would have his way, and said it must be tried. They cast lots, whereby the sausage was to carry wood, the mouse became cook, and the bird was to fetch water.

What happened? The sausage went out towards the wood, the bird lighted the fire, the mouse stayed by the pot and waited alone until the sausage came home and brought wood for next day. But the sausage stayed so long on the road that they both feared something was amiss, and the bird flew out a little way to meet it. Not far off it met a dog on the road who had swallowed the sausage. The bird charged the dog with an act of barefaced robbery, but in vain, for the dog said he had found forged letters on the sausage, on which account its life was forfeited to him.

The bird sadly took up the wood, flew home, and related what he had seen and heard. They were much troubled, but agreed to do their best and remain together. The bird therefore laid the cloth, and the

43

mouse made ready the food, and wanted to season it, and to get into the pot as the sausage used to do, and roll among the vegetables to flavour them; but before she got very far into the midst of them she was scalded, and lost her skin and her life in the attempt.

When the bird came home to dinner, no cook was there. In its distress the bird threw the wood about, called and searched, but no cook was to be found! Owing to his carelessness the wood caught fire and then the house caught fire. The bird hastened to fetch water. The bucket dropped from his claws into the well, and he fell down with it, and could not get out, and so he was drowned.

The Little Peasant

There once was a village where no one lived but really rich peasants, and just one poor one, whom they called the little peasant. He had not even a cow, still less any money to buy one, and yet he and his wife longed to have one. One day he said to her, "Listen, I've had an idea. Let's ask our friend the carpenter to make us a wooden calf, and paint it brown, so that it looks like any other calf, and in time it will certainly get big and be a cow."

His wife liked the idea, and their friend the carpenter cut and planed the calf, and painted it as it ought to be, and made it with its head hanging down as if it were eating.

Next morning when the cows were being driven out, the little peasant called the cowherd in and said, "Look, I have a little calf there, but it is still small and has to be carried." The cowherd said, "All right," and took it in his arms, carried it to the pasture and set it on the grass. The little calf always remained standing as if it were eating, and the cowherd said, "It will soon run about. Just look how it eats already!" At night when he was going to drive the herd home again, he said to the calf, "If you can stand there and eat your fill, you can also walk on your four legs. I'm not going to lug you home again in my arms."

But the little peasant stood at his door, and waited for his little calf,

and when the cowherd drove the cows through the village, and the calf was missing, he inquired where it was. The cowherd answered, "It is still standing out there. It would not stop eating to come with us."

The little peasant said, "Oh, but I must have my calf back again." Then they went back to the meadow together, but someone had stolen the calf, and it was gone. The cowherd said, "It must have run away." The peasant, however said, "Don't tell me that," and led the cowherd before the Mayor, who for his carelessness condemned the cowherd to give the peasant a cow, in place of the calf which had run away.

So now the little peasant and his wife had the cow for which they had so long wished, and they were heartily glad, but they had no food for it, so it soon had to be killed. They salted the meat, and the peasant went into the town to sell the hide, so that he might buy a new calf with the proceeds. On the way he passed a mill, and there sat a raven with broken wings, and out of pity he took him and wrapped him in the hide. As, however, the weather grew bad and there was a storm of rain and wind, he could go no further, and turned back to the mill and begged for shelter. The miller's wife was alone in the house, and said to the peasant, "Lay yourself on the straw there," and gave him a slice of bread with cheese on it. The peasant ate it, and lay down with his hide beside him, and the woman thought, "He is tired and has gone to sleep." In the meantime the parson came in; the miller's wife made him very welcome, and said, "My husband is out, so we'll have a feast." The peasant listened, and when he heard about feasting he was vexed that he had been forced to make shift with bread and cheese. Then the woman served up four different things: roast meat, salad, cakes, and wine.

Just as they were about to sit down and eat, there was a knocking outside. The woman said, "Oh, heavens! It is my husband!" She quickly hid the roast meat inside the tiled stove, the wine under the pillow, the salad on the bed, the cakes under it, and locked the parson in the cupboard. Then she opened the door for her husband, and said, "Thank heaven, you're back again! There's such a storm, it looks as if the world were coming to an end."

The miller saw the peasant lying on the straw, and asked, "What's that fellow doing there?"

"Ah," said the wife, "the poor knave came in the storm and rain, and begged for shelter, so I gave him a bit of bread and cheese, and showed him where the straw was."

The man said, "I have no objection, but be quick and get me something to eat."

The woman said, "But I have nothing but bread and cheese."

"That'll do," replied the husband. He looked at the peasant and said, "Come and eat some more with me."

The peasant did not need to be invited twice, but got up and ate. After this the miller saw the hide in which the raven was, lying on the ground, and asked, "What have you got there?"

"I have a soothsayer inside it," the peasant answered.

"Can he foretell anything to me?" said the miller.

"Why not?" answered the peasant. "But he only says four things, and the fifth he keeps to himself."

The miller was curious, and said, "Let him foretell the first thing."

Then the peasant pinched the raven's head, so that he croaked and made a noise like *krr, krr*. The miller said, "What did he say?"

The peasant answered, "First, he says that there's some wine hidden under the pillow."

"Bless me!" cried the miller, and went there and found the wine. "Now go on," said he.

The peasant made the raven croak again, and said, "Secondly, he says that there's some roast meat in the tiled stove."

"Upon my word!" cried the miller, and went there and found roast meat.

The peasant made the raven prophesy still more, and said, "Thirdly, he says that there's some salad on the bed."

"That'd be a fine thing!" cried the miller, and went there and found the salad.

At last the peasant pinched the raven once more till he croaked, and said, "Fourthly, he says that there are some cakes under the bed."

"I can't believe it!" cried the miller, and looked there, and found the cakes.

And now the two sat down to the table together, but the miller's wife was frightened to death, and went to bed and took all the keys with her. The miller longed to know the fifth thing, and the little peasant said, "First, we will quickly eat the four things, for the fifth is something bad."

So they ate, and after that they bargained over how much the miller was to give for the fifth prophecy, until they agreed on three hundred thalers. Then the peasant once more pinched the raven's head till he croaked loudly. The miller asked, "What did he say?" The peasant replied, "He says that the Devil is hiding there in the cupboard."

"The Devil must go out," said the miller. The woman was forced to give up the keys, and the peasant unlocked the cupboard. The parson ran out as fast as he could, and the miller said, "It was true; I saw the black rascal with my own eyes."

Next morning by daybreak the peasant had made off with the three hundred thalers.

Once home the little peasant gradually launched out; he built a beautiful house, and the rich peasants said, "The little peasant has certainly been to the place where golden snow falls, and people carry the gold home in shovels."

Then the little peasant was brought before the Mayor, and bidden to say how he had got his wealth. He answered, "I sold my cow's hide in the town for three hundred thalers."

When the other peasants heard that, they too wished to enjoy this great profit. They ran home, killed all their cows, and stripped off their hides in order to sell them in the town to the best advantage. The Mayor, however, said "My servant must go first." When she came to the merchant in the town, he did not give her more than two thalers for a hide, and when the others came, he gave them less, and said, "What can I do with all these hides?"

Then the peasants were furious with the little peasant for having stolen a march on them. They wanted to take vengeance on him, and accused him of treachery before the Mayor. The innocent little peasant was unanimously sentenced to death. He was to be rolled into the water, in a barrel pierced full of holes. He was led forth, and a priest was brought to say a mass for his soul. The others were all obliged to retire to a distance, and when the peasant looked at the priest, he recognized the man who had supped with the miller's wife. He said to him, "I set you free from the cupboard. Set me free from the barrel."

At this same moment up came, with a flock of sheep, the very shepherd who, as the peasant knew, had long been wishing to be Mayor, so he cried with all his might, "No, I will not do it; if the whole world insists on it, I will not do it!"

The shepherd hearing this, came up to him, and asked, "What's all this? What is it you will not do?"

"They want to make me Mayor," said the peasant, "if only I'll put myself in the barrel, but I will not do it."

The shepherd said, "If nothing more than that is needful in order to be Mayor, I'd get into the barrel at once."

"If you'll get in," said the peasant, "you'll be Mayor."

The shepherd was willing, and got in, and the peasant shut the top down on him; then he took the shepherd's flock for himself, and drove it away. The parson went to the crowd, and declared that the mass had been said. Then they came and rolled the barrel towards the water.

When the barrel began to roll, the shepherd cried, "I am quite willing to be Mayor." The people all believed that it was the peasant who was saying this, and answered, "First you can have a look round down below there," and they rolled the barrel into the water.

After that the crowd went home, and as they were entering the village, the little peasant came quietly in, driving a flock of sheep and looking quite contented. Then the peasants were astonished, and said, "Peasant, where have you come from? Have you come out of the water?"

"Yes," replied the peasant. "I sank deep, deep down, until at last I got to the bottom. I pushed the bottom out of the barrel, and crept out, and there were pretty meadows on which a number of lambs were feeding, and from thence I brought this flock away with me."

"Are there any more there?" asked the peasants.

"Oh, yes," said he, "more than I could do anything with."

Then the peasants made up their minds that they too would fetch some sheep for themselves, a flock apiece, but the Mayor said, "I come first." So they went to the water together, and just then there were some small fleecy clouds in the blue sky, which are called little lambs,

and they were reflected in the water, whereupon the peasants cried, "We already see the sheep down below!"

The Mayor pressed forward and said, "I'll go down first, and look about me, and if things promise well I'll call you."

So he jumped in. *Splash* went the water; he made a sound as if he were calling them, and the whole crowd plunged in after him as one man. Then the entire village was dead, and the little peasant, as sole heir, became rich.

The Bremen Town-Musicians

A certain man had a donkey, which had carried sacks of corn to the mill faithfully for very many long years, but his strength was going, and he was growing more and more unfit for work. Then his master began to consider how he might best save his keep; but the donkey, seeing that trouble was brewing, ran away and set out on the road to Bremen. "There," he thought, "I can surely be a town-musician."

When he had walked some distance, he found a hound lying on the road, panting like one who had run till he was tired.

"What are you panting so for, you big fellow?" asked the donkey.

"Ah," replied the hound, "as I am old, and daily grow weaker, and can no longer hunt, my master wanted to kill me, so I ran off; but now how am I to earn my bread?"

"I tell you what," said the donkey, "I am going to Bremen, and shall be a town-musician there; go with me and be a musician too. I will play the lute, and you shall beat the kettledrum."

The hound agreed, and on they went.

Before long they came to a cat, sitting on the path, with a face like three rainy days! "Now then, old moggy, what's gone wrong with you?" asked the donkey.

"Who can be merry when his neck is in danger?" answered the cat. "Because I'm getting old, and my teeth are worn to stumps, and I prefer to sit by the fire and purr, rather than hunt mice, my mistress wanted to drown me, so I ran away. But now where am I to go?"

"Go with us to Bremen. You caterwaul at night, so you can be a town-musician."

The cat thought well of it, and went with them. After this the three runaways came to a farmyard, where the cock was sitting upon the gate, crowing with all his might.

"Your crow goes through and through one," said the donkey. "What's the matter?"

"I have been foretelling fine weather, because it is the day on which Our Lady washes the Christ Child's little shirts, and wants to dry them," said the cock; "but guests are coming on Sunday, so the housewife has told the cook to make me into a soup tomorrow, and this evening I am to have my head cut off. Now I am crowing with all my might while I can."

"You had better come away with us, Redcomb," said the donkey. "We are going to Bremen. You can find a better fate than death there. You have a good voice, and if we make music together it must have some quality!"

The cock agreed to this plan, and all four went on together. They could not, however, reach the city of Bremen in one day, and in the evening they came to a forest where they decided to pass the night. The donkey and the hound lay down under a large tree, the cat and the cock settled themselves in the branches; but the cock flew right to the top, where he was safest. Before he went to sleep he looked round on all four sides, and thought he saw a light in the distance; so he called out to his companions that there must be a house not far off. The donkey said, "If so, we had better get up and go on, for there's no real shelter here." The hound thought that a few bones with some meat on would do him good!

So they made their way to the place where the light was, and soon saw it shine brighter and grow larger, until they came to a robber's well-lighted house. The donkey, as the biggest, went to the window and looked in.

"What do you see, old jackass?" asked the cock.

"What do I see?" answered the donkey. "A table covered with

good things to eat and drink, and robbers sitting at it enjoying themselves."

"That would just suit us," said the cock.

"Yes, how I wish we were in there!" said the donkey.

Then the animals discussed how they could drive away the robbers, and at last they thought of a plan. The donkey was to put his forefeet upon the window-ledge, the hound was to jump on the donkey's back, the cat was to climb upon the dog, and lastly the cock was to fly up and perch upon the head of the cat.

When this was done, at a given signal they began to perform their music together: the donkey brayed, the hound barked, the cat mewed, and the cock crowed; then they burst through the window into the room, shattering the glass! At this horrible din, the robbers sprang up, convinced that a ghost had come in, and fled in a great fright out into the forest. The four companions sat down at the table, well content with what was left, and ate as if they were going to fast for a month.

As soon as the four minstrels had done, they put out the light, and each sought a sleeping-place to suit him. The donkey lay down upon some straw in the yard, the hound behind the door, the cat upon the hearth near the warm ashes, and the cock perched upon a beam of the roof; and being tired with their long walk, they soon went to sleep.

When it was past midnight, and the robbers saw from afar that the light was no longer burning in their house, and all appeared quiet, the captain said, "We ought not to have let ourselves be frightened out of our wits!" and ordered one of them to go and search the house.

The messenger, finding all quiet, went into the kitchen to light a candle, and, taking the glistening fiery eyes of the cat for live coals, he held a match to them to light it. But the cat did not understand the joke, and flew in his face, spitting and scratching. He was dreadfully frightened, and ran to the back door, but the dog, who lay there, sprang up and bit his leg; and as he ran across the yard by the manure heap, the donkey gave him a smart kick with its hind hoof. The cock, awakened by the noise, crowed loudly from the beam, "Cock-a-doodle-doo!"

Then the robber ran back as fast as he could to his captain, and said, "Ah, there is a horrible witch sitting in the house, who spat on me and

scratched my face with her long claws; and by the door stands a man with a knife, who stabbed me in the leg; and in the yard there lies a black monster, who beat me with a wooden club; and above, upon the roof, sits the judge, who called out, 'Bring the rogue here to me!' so I got away as well as I could."

After this the robbers did not trust themselves in the house again; but it suited the four musicians of Bremen so well that they never wanted to leave it.

Mother Hulda

There was once a widow who had two daughters, one of whom was pretty and industrious, while the other was ugly and idle. But she was much fonder of the ugly and idle one, because she was her own daughter; and the other, who was a stepdaughter, was obliged to do all the work, and be the Cinderella of the house. Every day the poor girl had to sit in the street by a well, and spin and spin till her fingers bled.

One day the shuttle was marked with her blood, so she dipped it in the well, to wash the mark off; but it dropped out of her hand and fell to the bottom. She began to weep, and ran to her stepmother and told her of the mishap. But her stepmother scolded her sharply, and said harshly, "Since you have let the shuttle fall in, you must fetch it out again."

So the girl went back to the well, and did not know what to do; and in the sorrow of her heart she jumped into the well to get the shuttle. She became unconscious; and when she came to herself again, she was in a lovely meadow where the sun was shining and thousands of flowers were growing. Along this meadow she went, and at last came to a baker's oven full of bread, and the bread cried out, "Oh, take me out! Take me out or I shall burn; I have been baked a long time!"

So she went up to it, and took out all the loaves one after another

57

with the bread-shovel. After that she went on till she came to a tree covered with apples, which called out to her, "Oh, shake me! Shake me! My apples are all ripe!" So she shook the tree till the apples fell like rain, and went on shaking till they were all down, and when she had gathered them into a heap, she went on her way.

At last she came to a little house, out of which an old woman peered; but she had such large teeth that the girl was frightened, and was about to run away.

But the old woman called out to her, "What are you afraid of, dear child? Stay with me. If you will do all the work in the house properly, I shall be pleased with you. Only you must take care to make my bed well, and to shake it thoroughly till the feathers fly – for then there is snow on the earth. I am Mother Hulda."

As the old woman spoke so kindly to her, the girl took courage and agreed to enter her service. She did everything to the satisfaction of her mistress, and always shook her bed so vigorously that the feathers flew like snowflakes. So she had a pleasant life with her: never an angry word, and boiled or roast meat every day.

She stayed some time with Mother Hulda, and then she became sad. At first she did not know what was the matter with her, but realized at length that it was homesickness: although she was many thousand times better off here than at home, still she had a longing to be there. At last she said to the old woman, "I long for home; and though I am happy here, I cannot stay any longer; I must go up again to my own people."

Mother Hulda said, "I am glad that you long for home, and as you have served me so well I myself will take you up again."

She took her by the hand, and led her to a large door. The door was opened, and as the maiden stood beneath the doorway a heavy shower of golden rain fell, and all the gold remained sticking to her, so that she was completely covered with it.

"You shall have that because you are so industrious," said Mother Hulda, and at the same time she gave her back the shuttle which she had let fall into the well. Then the door closed, and the maiden found herself up above upon the earth, not far from her stepmother's house.

And as she went into the yard the cock was standing by the well-side and cried,

> *"Cock-a-doodle-doo!*
> *Your golden girl's come back to you!"*

So she went in to her stepmother, and as she arrived thus covered with gold, she was well received, both by her and by her sister.

As soon as the stepmother heard how the girl had come by so much wealth she was very anxious to obtain the same good luck for the ugly and lazy daughter. She had to seat herself by the well and spin; and in order that her shuttle might be stained with blood she stuck her hand into a thorn bush and pricked her finger. Then she threw her shuttle into the well, and jumped in after it.

She came, like her sister, to the beautiful meadow and walked along the very same path. When she got to the oven the bread again cried, "Oh, take me out! Take me out or I shall burn; I have been baked a long time!" But the lazy thing answered, "I'm not going to make myself dirty!" and on she went. Soon she came to the apple tree which cried, "Oh, shake me! Shake me! My apples are all ripe!" But she answered, "I like that! One of them might fall on my head," and so went on.

When she came to Mother Hulda's house she was not afraid, for she had already heard of her big teeth, and she hired herself to her immediately.

The first day she forced herself to work diligently, and obeyed Mother Hulda when she told her to do anything, for she was thinking of all the gold that she would give her. But on the second day she began to be lazy, and on the third day still more so, and then she would not get up in the morning at all. Neither did she make Mother Hulda's bed as she ought, and did not shake it to make the feathers fly up. Mother Hulda was soon tired of this, and gave her notice to leave. The lazy girl was willing enough to go and thought that now the golden rain would come. Mother Hulda led her to the great door; but while she was standing beneath it, instead of the gold a big kettleful of soot was emptied over her.

"That is the reward for your service," said Mother Hulda, and shut the door.

So the lazy girl went home, smothered in soot, and the cock by the well-side, as soon as he saw her, cried out,

"Cock-a-doodle-doo!
Your sooty girl's come back to you!"

The soot stuck fast to her, and she never got rid of it as long as she lived.

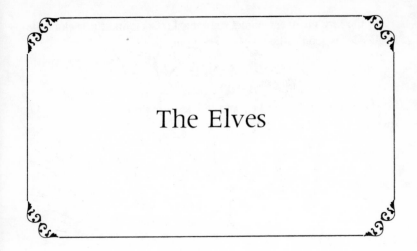

The Elves

First Story

There was once a poor servant-girl, who was industrious and swept the house every day, and emptied her sweepings on the great heap in front of the door.

One morning she found a letter on this heap, and as she could not read, she put her broom in the corner, and took the letter to her master and mistress. To their surprise it was an invitation from the elves, who asked the girl to be godmother to a child of theirs at its christening. The girl did not know what to do, but at length, after much persuasion, and as they told her that it was not right to refuse an invitation of this kind, she consented.

Then three elves came and conducted her to a hollow mountain, where the little folks lived. Everything there was small, but more elegant and beautiful than can be described. The baby's mother lay in a bed of black ebony ornamented with pearls, the coverlets were embroidered with gold, the cradle was of ivory, the bath of gold. The girl stood as godmother, and then wanted to go home again, but the little elves urgently entreated her to stay three days with them. So she stayed, and passed the time in pleasure and gaiety, and the little folks did all they could to make her happy.

At last she set out on her way home. First they filled her pockets to the brim with money, and after that they led her out of the mountain again.

When she got home she took the broom, which was still standing in the corner, in her hand and began to sweep. Then some strangers came out of the house, who asked her who she was, and what business she had there? And she had not, as she thought, been three days with the little men in the mountains, but seven years, and in the meantime her former masters had died.

Second Story

A certain mother's child had been taken away out of its cradle by the elves, and a changeling with a large head and staring eyes, which would do nothing but eat and drink, laid in its place. In her trouble the mother went to her neighbour, and asked her advice. The neighbour said that she was to carry the changeling into the kitchen, set it down on the hearth, light a fire, and boil some water in two eggshells. This would make the changeling laugh, and if he laughed, all would be over with him.

The woman did everything that her neighbour bade her. When she put the eggshells full of water on the fire, the imp said,

"Though I am old as the oldest tree,
Cooking in an eggshell never did I see."

And he began to laugh at it. While he was laughing, a host of little elves suddenly came in. They brought the right child, set it down on the hearth, and took the changeling away with them.

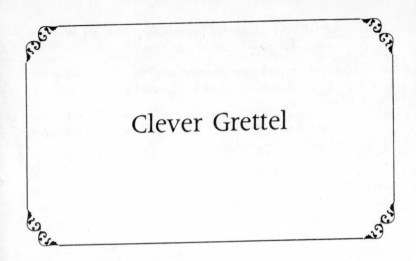

Clever Grettel

There was once a cook named Grettel, who wore shoes with red rosettes, and when she went out in them, she turned herself this way and that, and thought, "You certainly are a pretty girl!" And when she came home she drank, in her gladness of heart, a draught of wine; and as wine gives an appetite, she sampled the best of whatever she was cooking, and said, "The cook must know how the food tastes."

Her master said to her one day, "Grettel, a guest is coming this evening. Prepare me two fowls in your best style."

"I will see to it, master," answered Grettel. She killed two fowls, scalded them, plucked them, put them on the spit, and towards evening set them before the fire to roast. The fowls began to turn brown, and were nearly ready, but the guest had not yet arrived. Then Grettel called out to her master, "If the guest does not come, I must take the fowls away from the fire, but it will be a sin and a shame if they are not eaten directly, while they are so juicy."

"I will run myself, and fetch my guest," said her master.

When the master had turned his back, Grettel laid the spit with the fowls on one side, and thought, "Standing in front of a hot fire has made me thirsty. Who knows when they will come? Meanwhile, I will run into the cellar, and take a drink." She ran down, filled a jug, said, "Your health, Grettel," took a long drink, and yet another hearty draught.

66

Then she went and put the fowls down again before the fire, basted them, and drove the spit merrily round. The roast meat smelt so good that Grettel thought, "Something might be wrong; it ought to be tasted!"

She touched the meat with her finger, licked it and said, "Ah, how good fowls are! It certainly is a sin and a shame that they are not eaten directly!"

She ran to the window, to see if the master was coming, but she saw no one, and went back to the fowls and thought, "One of the wings is burning! I had better take it off and eat it."

So she cut it off, ate it, and enjoyed it, and when she had done, she thought, "The other must come off too, or else master will see that something is missing."

When the two wings were eaten, she went and looked for her master. No sign of him. It suddenly occurred to her, "Who knows? Perhaps they aren't coming at all, and have stopped somewhere." Then she said, "Well, Grettel, enjoy yourself; one fowl has been cut into; take another drink, and eat it up entirely; when it is eaten you will have some peace. Why should God's good gifts be spoilt?"

So she ran into the cellar again, took an enormous drink and ate up the one chicken with gusto. When she had gobbled it up, and still her master did not come, Grettel looked at the other and said, "Where one is, the other should be likewise; the two go together. I think if I were to take another draught it would do me no harm." So she took another hearty drink, and let the second chicken rejoin the first.

Just as she was thoroughly enjoying her meal, her master returned and cried, "Hurry, Grettel, the guest is on his way!"

"Yes, sir, I'll soon serve up," answered Grettel.

Meantime the master looked to see that the table was properly laid, and took the great knife, wherewith he was going to carve the chickens, and sharpened it on the steps. Presently the guest came, and knocked politely and courteously at the house-door. Grettel ran to see who was there, and when she saw the guest, she put her finger to her lips and said, "Hush! Get away as quickly as you can; if my master catches you it will be the worse for you. He certainly asked you to supper, but his

67

intention is to cut off your two ears. Just listen how he is sharpening the knife for it!"

The guest heard the sharpening, and hurried down the steps again as fast as he could. With all speed, Grettel ran screaming to her master, and cried, "You have invited a fine guest!"

"Eh, why, Grettel? What do you mean?"

"Yes," said she, "he has taken the chickens which I was just going to serve up, off the dish, and has run away with them!"

"That's a nice trick!" said her master, and lamented the fine chickens. "If only he had left me one, so that I had something to eat." He called to him to stop, but the guest pretended not to hear. Then he ran after him with the knife still in his hand, crying, "Just one, just one," meaning that the guest should leave him just one chicken, and not take both. The guest, however, thought otherwise – that he was to give up one of his ears, and ran as if fire were burning under him, in order to take both ears home with him.

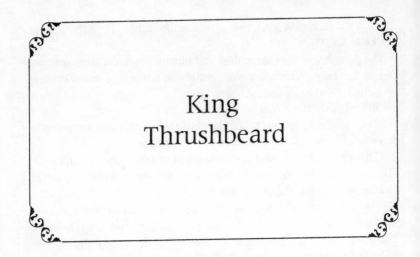

King
Thrushbeard

A King had a daughter who was more beautiful than words could tell, but so proud and haughty that no suitor was good enough for her. She sent away one after the other, and ridiculed them as well.

One day the King gave a great feast and invited to it, from far and near, all the marriageable young men. They were marshalled in a row according to their rank and standing. First came the kings, then the grand-dukes, then the princes, the earls, the barons, and the gentry. The King's daughter was led through the ranks, but to every one she made some objection: one was too fat, "Round as a barrel," she said. Another was too tall, "Long and thin has little in." The third was too short, "Short and thick is never quick." The fourth was too pale, "As pale as death." The fifth too red, "A fighting-cock." The sixth was not straight enough, "A green log dried behind the stove."

So she had something to say against every one, but she made herself especially merry over a good king who was one of the first in the row, and whose chin had grown a little crooked.

"Well," she cried and laughed, "he has a chin like a thrush's beak!" and from that time he got the name of King Thrushbeard.

But the old King, when he saw that his daughter did nothing but mock and despise all the suitors gathered there, was very angry, and

swore that she should have for her husband the very first beggar that came to his doors.

A few days afterwards a fiddler came and sang beneath the windows trying to earn a little money. When the King heard him he said, "Let him come up."

So the fiddler came in, in his dirty, ragged clothes, and sang before the King and his daughter, and then he asked for a trifling gift. The King said, "Your song has pleased me so well that I will give you my daughter to be your wife."

The King's daughter shuddered, but the King said, "I have taken an oath to give you to the very first beggar-man, and I will keep it." All she could say was in vain; the priest was brought, and she had to let herself be wedded to the fiddler on the spot. When that was done the King said, "It is not proper for you, a beggar-woman, to stay any longer in my palace, so away you go with your husband."

The beggar-man led her out by the hand, and she was obliged to walk away on foot with him. When they came to a large forest she asked,

> *"Oh, whose is this forest so thick and so fine ?"*

And the echo answered,

> *"It is King Thrushbeard's and might have been thine."*

"Ah, unhappy girl that I am, if I had but taken King Thrushbeard!" Afterwards they came to a meadow, and she asked again.

> *"Oh, whose is this meadow so green and so fine ?"*

And the echo answered,

> *"It is King Thrushbeard's and might have been thine."*

"Ah, unhappy girl that I am, if I had but taken King Thrushbeard!" Then they came to a large town, and she asked again,

> *"Oh, whose is this city so great and so fine ?"*

And the echo answered,

> *"It is King Thrushbeard's and might have been thine."*

"Ah, unhappy girl that I am, if I had but taken King Thrushbeard!"

"It does not please me," said the fiddler, "to hear you always wishing for another husband; am I not good enough for you?"

At last they came to a very little hut, and she said, "Oh, goodness! what a small house; to whom does this miserable, mean hovel belong?"

"This is my house and yours," the fiddler answered, "where we shall live together."

She had to stoop in order to go in at the low door.

"Where are the servants?" asked the King's daughter.

"What servants?" answered the beggar-man. "Whatever you want done you must do yourself. Just make a fire at once, and put on water to cook my supper."

But the king's daughter knew nothing about lighting fires or cooking, and the beggar-man had to lend a hand himself to get anything done. When they had finished their scanty meal they went to bed; but he forced her to get up early in the morning to do the housework.

For a few days they lived in this way until they had finished all their provisions. Then the man said, "Wife, we cannot go on any longer eating and drinking and earning nothing. You must weave baskets." He went out, cut some osiers from the willow trees, and brought them home. She began to weave, but the tough osiers hurt her delicate hands.

"I see that this won't do," said the man; "you had better spin; perhaps you can do that better."

She sat down and tried to spin, but the hard thread soon cut her soft fingers till they bled.

"See," said the man, "you're fit for no sort of work; I've made a bad bargain with you. I'll try to start a business with pots and earthenware; you must sit in the market-place and sell the ware."

"Alas," thought she, "if any of the people from my father's kingdom come to the market and see me sitting there, selling, how they will mock me." But it was no use: she had to obey unless she chose to die of hunger.

The first time she did well, for the people were glad to buy her wares because she was good-looking, and they paid her what she asked. In fact many even gave her the money and left the pots with her as well. So they lived on what she had earned as long as it lasted. Then the

73

husband bought a lot of new crockery. With this she sat down at the corner of the market-place, and set it out round about her ready for sale.

Suddenly a drunken hussar came galloping along, and he rode right among the pots and broke them into a thousand bits. She began to weep, and did not know what to do for fear.

"Alas! what will happen to me?" she cried. "What will my husband say to this?" She ran home and told him of the misfortune.

"Who would be silly enough to sit at a corner of the market-place with crockery?" said the man. "Stop crying. I see very well that you aren't fit for ordinary work, so I have been to our King's palace and have asked whether they need a kitchen-maid, and they will take you. That way you will at least get your food for nothing."

The King's daughter was now a kitchen-maid, and had to be at the cook's beck and call, and do the dirtiest work. In both her pockets she fastened a little jar, in which she took home her share of the leavings, and upon this they lived.

It so happened that the wedding of the King's eldest son was to be celebrated, so the poor woman went upstairs and stood behind the door of the hall to look on. When all the candles were lit, and the guests, each more beautiful than the other, entered, and all was pomp and splendour, she thought of her lot with a sad heart, and cursed the pride and haughtiness which had humbled her and brought her to such poverty.

The smell of the delicious dishes which were being taken in and out reached her, and now and then the servants threw her a few morsels of them: these she put in her jars to take home.

All at once the King's son entered, clothed in velvet and silk, with gold chains about his neck. When he saw the beautiful woman standing by the door he seized her by the hand, and would have danced with her; but she refused and shrank back with fear, for she saw that it was King Thrushbeard, the suitor whom she had driven away with scorn. Her struggles were of no avail; he drew her into the hall; but the string by which her pockets were hung broke, the pots fell down, the soup ran out, and the scraps were scattered all about. And when the people saw it, they shouted with laughter and derision, and she was so ashamed that she wished she could sink into the ground.

She sprang to the door and would have run away, but on the stairs a man caught her and brought her back; and when she looked at him it was King Thrushbeard. He said to her kindly, "Do not be afraid. I and the fiddler who has been living with you in that wretched hovel are one. For love of you I disguised myself so; and I also was the hussar who rode through your crockery. This was all done to humble your proud spirit, and to punish you for the insolence with which you mocked me."

Then she wept bitterly and said, "I have done great wrong, and am not worthy to be your wife."

"Be comforted," he said, "those evil days are past; now we will celebrate our real wedding."

Then the maids-in-waiting came and put on her rich clothing, and her father and his whole court came and wished her happiness in her marriage with King Thrushbeard. Her joy began in earnest. I wish you and I had been there too.

Our Lady's Child

Hard by a great forest dwelt a woodcutter with his wife. They had an only child, a little girl of three years old. They were so poor that they had very little to eat.

One morning the woodcutter went out sorrowfully to his work in the forest, and while he was cutting wood, suddenly there stood before him a tall and beautiful woman with a crown of shining stars on her head, who said to him, "I am the Virgin Mary, mother of the child Jesus. You are poor and needy; bring your child to me. I will take her with me and be her mother, and care for her."

The woodcutter obeyed, brought his child, and gave her to Our Lady, who took her up to heaven with her. There the child fared well, ate sugar-cakes, and drank sweet milk, and her clothes were of gold, and the little angels played with her. When she was fourteen years of age, Our Lady called her one day and said, "Dear child, I am about to make a long journey, so take into your keeping the keys of the thirteen doors of heaven. Twelve of these you may open, and behold the glory which is within them, but the thirteenth, to which this little key belongs, is forbidden you. Beware of opening it, or you will bring misery on yourself."

The girl promised to be obedient, and when Our Lady was gone, she began to examine the dwellings of the kingdom of heaven. Each day she opened one of them, until she had made the round of the twelve. In each of them sat one of the Apostles in the midst of a great light, and she rejoiced in all the magnificence and splendour, and the little angels who always accompanied her rejoiced with her.

Then the forbidden door alone remained, and she felt a great desire to know what could be hidden behind it, and said to the angels, "I will not quite open it, and I will nòt go inside it, but I will unlock it so that we can just see a little through the opening."

"Oh, no," said the little angels, "that would be a sin. For Our Lady has forbidden it, and it might easily cause you unhappiness."

Then she was silent, but the desire in her heart was not stilled, but gnawed there and tormented her, and gave her no rest. And once when the angels had all gone out, she thought, "Now I am quite alone, and I could peep in. No one will ever know."

She sought out the key, put it in the lock and turned it. Then the door sprang open, and she saw there the Trinity sitting in fire and splendour. She stayed there awhile, and looked at everything in amazement; then she touched the light with her finger, and her finger became quite golden. Immediately a great fear fell on her. She shut the door violently, and ran away. Nothing could stop her terror, and her heart beat continually and would not be still; the gold too stayed on her finger, and would not go away, though she rubbed it and washed it over and over again.

It was not long before Our Lady came back from her journey. She called the girl and asked to have the keys of heaven back. When the maiden gave her the bunch, Our Lady looked into her eyes and said, "Have you not opened the thirteenth door also ?"

"No," she replied.

Then Our Lady laid her hand on the girl's heart, and felt how it beat and beat, and saw clearly that she had disobeyed her and opened the door. Then she said once again, "Are you certain you did not open it ?"

"Yes," said the girl for the second time.

Then Our Lady saw the finger which had become golden from touching the fire of heaven, and knew that the child had sinned, and said for the third time, "Have you opened it ?"

"No," said the girl for the third time.

Then said Our Lady, "You have not obeyed me, and besides that you have lied. You are no longer worthy to be in heaven."

Then the girl fell into a deep sleep, and when she awoke she lay on the earth below, in the midst of a wilderness. She wanted to cry out, but could utter no sound. She sprang up and tried to run away, but wherever she turned, she was continually held back by thick hedges of thorns through which she could not break. In the wilderness in which she was imprisoned there stood an old hollow tree, and this had to be her dwelling-place. Into this she crept when night came, and here she slept. Here, too, she found a shelter from storm and rain, but it was a miserable life and bitterly did she weep when she remembered how happy she had been in heaven, and how the angels had played with her. Roots and wild berries were her only food, and for these she sought as far as she could go.

In autumn she picked up the fallen nuts and leaves, and carried them into the hole. The nuts were her food in winter, and when snow and ice came, she crept among the leaves like a poor little animal that she might not freeze. Before long her clothes were all torn, and rag by rag fell off her. As soon, however, as the sun shone warm again, she went out and sat in front of the tree, and her long hair covered her like a mantle. Thus she sat year after year, and felt the pain and misery of the world.

One day, when the trees were once more clothed in fresh green, the King of the country was hunting in the forest, and followed a roe, which had fled into a thicket. He got off his horse, tore the bushes asunder, and cut himself a path with his sword. When he had at last forced his way through, he saw a wonderfully beautiful maiden sitting under a tree. She sat there and was entirely covered with her golden hair down to her very feet.

He stood still and looked at her full of surprise. Then he asked her, "Who are you? Why are you sitting here in the wilderness?"

But she gave no answer, for she could not open her mouth.

The King continued, "Will you go with me to my castle?"

Then she just nodded her head a little. The King took her in his arms, carried her to his horse, and rode home with her, and when he reached

the royal castle he caused her to be dressed in beautiful garments, and gave her all things in abundance. Although she could not speak, she was still so beautiful and charming that he began to love her with all his heart, and it was not long before he married her.

After a year or so had passed, the Queen brought a son into the world. Thereupon Our Lady appeared to her in the night when she lay in her bed alone, and said, "If you will tell the truth and confess that you unlocked the forbidden door, I will give you back your speech, but if you persevere in your sin, and deny obstinately, I will take your new-born child away with me."

Then the Queen was able to speak, but she remained stubborn and said, "No, I did not open the forbidden door"; and Our Lady took the new-born child from her arms and vanished with it. Next morning, when the child was not to be found, it was whispered among the people that the Queen had killed her own child. She heard all this and could say nothing to the contrary, but the King would not believe it, for he loved her so much.

When a year had gone by the Queen again bore a son, and in the night Our Lady again came to her, and said, "If you will confess that you opened the forbidden door, I will give your child back and untie your tongue; but if you continue in sin and deny it, I will take away with me this new child also."

Then the Queen again said, "No, I did not open the forbidden door"; and Our Lady took the child out of her arms, and went away with him.

Next morning, when this child also had disappeared, the people declared quite loudly that the Queen had killed him, and the King's councillors demanded that she should be brought to justice. The King, however, loved her so dearly that he would not believe it, and commanded the councillors under pain of death to say no more about it.

The following year the Queen have birth to a beautiful little daughter, and for the third time Our Lady appeared to her in the night. She said, "Follow me." She took the Queen by the hand and led her to Heaven, and showed her there her two eldest children, who smiled at her and were playing with the ball of the world. When the Queen rejoiced to see them, Our Lady said, "Is your heart not yet softened? If you will own that you opened the forbidden door, I will give you back your two little sons."

But the third time the Queen answered, "No, I did not open the forbidden door." Then Our Lady let her sink down to earth once more, and took her third child from her.

Next morning, when the loss was reported abroad, all the people cried loudly, "The Queen is a murderess! She must be judged," and the King was no longer able to restrain his councillors. Thereupon a trial was held, and as she could not answer, and defend herself, she was condemned to be burnt alive. When she was bound fast to the stake, the hard ice of pride melted, her heart was moved by repentance, and she thought, "If only I could confess before my death that I opened the door!"

Then her voice came back to her, and she cried out loudly, "Yes, Mary, I did it"; and straightaway rain fell from the sky and extinguished the flames of fire, and a light broke forth above her, and Our Lady descended with the two little sons by her side, and the new-born daughter in her arms. She spoke to her, and said, "He who repents his sin and confesses it is at once forgiven."

Then she gave her the three children, untied her tongue, and granted her happiness for her whole life.

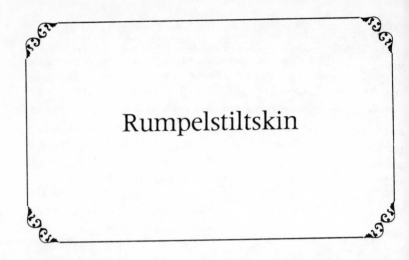

Rumpelstiltskin

Once there was a miller who was poor, but he had a beautiful daughter. Now it happened that he had to go and speak to the King, and in order to make himself appear important he said to him, "I have a daughter who can spin straw into gold."

The King said to the miller, "That is an art which pleases me well. If your daughter is as clever as you say, bring her tomorrow to my palace, and I will try what she can do."

And when the girl was brought to him he took her into a room full of straw, gave her a spinning-wheel and a reel, and said, "Now set to work, and if by tomorrow morning early you have not spun this straw into gold, you must die." Thereupon he locked up the room, and left her in it alone.

So there sat the poor miller's daughter, and for the life of her she did not know what to do; she had no idea how straw could be spun into gold, and she grew more and more miserable, until at last she began to weep.

But all at once the door opened, and in came a little man, and said, "Good evening, Mistress Miller; why are you crying so?"

"Alas!" answered the girl. "I have to spin straw into gold, and I do not know how to do it."

"What will you give me," said the manikin, "if I do it for you?"

"My necklace," said the girl.

The little man took the necklace, seated himself in front of the wheel, and sang,

> *"Round about, round about, lo and behold!*
> *Reel away, reel away, straw into gold,"*

and "whirr, whirr, whirr" three turns, and the reel was full. Then he put another on, and whirr, whirr, whirr, three times round, and the second was full too. And so it went on until the morning, when all the straw was spun, and all the reels were full of gold.

By daybreak the King was already there, and when he saw the gold he was astonished and delighted, but he became only more greedy. He had the miller's daughter taken into a much larger room full of straw, and commanded her to spin that also in one night if she valued her life.

The girl was at her wits' end and began to sob, when the door again opened, and the little man appeared, and said, "What will you give me if I spin the straw into gold for you?"

"The ring on my finger," answered the girl.

The little man took the ring, again began to turn the wheel and by morning had spun all the straw into glittering gold.

The King rejoiced beyond measure at the sight, but still he had not gold enough; and he had the miller's daughter taken into a still larger room full of straw, and said, "You must spin this, too, in the course of this night; but if you succeed, you shall be my Queen." "Even if she be a miller's daughter," thought he, "I could not find a richer wife in the whole world."

When the girl was alone the dwarf came again for the third time, and said, "What will you give me if I spin the straw for you this time also?"

"I have nothing left that I could give," answered the girl.

"Then promise me, if you should become Queen, your first child."

"Who knows whether that will ever happen?" thought the miller's daughter; and not knowing how else to help herself in this strait, she promised the little man what he wanted, and for that he once more spun the straw into gold.

83

When the King came in the morning and found all as he had wished, he took her in marriage, and the pretty miller's daughter became a Queen.

A year after, she had a beautiful child, and she never gave a thought to the dwarf. But suddenly he came into her room, and said, "Now give me what you promised."

The Queen was horror-struck, and offered the dwarf all the riches of the kingdom if he would leave her the child. But the dwarf said, "No, something that is living is dearer to me than all the treasures in the world." The Queen began to weep and cry, so that he pitied her. "I will give you three days," said he. "If by that time you find out my name, then you shall keep your child."

So the Queen thought the whole night of all the names that she had ever heard, and she sent a messenger over the country to inquire far and wide for any other names that there might be. When the manikin came the next day, she began with Caspar, Melchior, Balthazar, and said all the names she knew, one after another; but to every one the little man said, "That's not my name."

On the second day she had inquiries made in the neighbourhood as to the names of the people there, and she repeated to the dwarf the most uncommon and curious. "Perhaps your name is Shortribs, or Sheepshanks, or Lacelog?" but he always answered, "That's not my name."

On the third day the messenger came back again, and said, "I have not been able to find a single new name, but as I came to a high mountain at the end of the forest, there I saw a little house, and before the house a fire was burning, and round about the fire a ridiculous little man was jumping. He hopped upon one leg, and shouted,

> "Today I'll brew and then I'll bake.
> Tomorrow I shall the Queen's child take.
> How lucky it is that nobody knows
> My name is Rumpelstiltskin."

You can imagine how glad the Queen was when she heard the name! And when soon afterwards the little man came in, and asked, "Now

Mistress Queen, what is my name?" at first she said, "Is your name Conrad?"

"No."

"Is your name Nicholas?"

"No."

"Perhaps your name is Rumpelstiltskin?"

"The devil has told you that! The devil has told you that!" cried the little man, and in his anger he plunged his right foot so deep into the earth that his whole leg went in; and then in rage he pulled at his left leg so hard with both hands that he tore himself in two.

The Hut
in the Forest

A poor woodcutter lived with his wife and three daughters in a little hut on the edge of a lonely forest. One morning as he was about to go to his work, he said to his wife, "Let my dinner be brought into the forest to me by our eldest daughter, or I shall never get my work done; and in order that she may not miss her way," he added, "I will take a bag of millet with me and strew the seeds on the path."

When, therefore, the sun was just above the centre of the forest, the girl set out on her way with a bowl of soup, but the field-sparrows and the wood-sparrows, larks and finches, blackbirds and siskins had picked up the millet long before, and the girl could not find the track. So, trusting to chance, she went on and on, until the sun sank and night began to fall. The trees rustled in the darkness, the owls hooted, and she began to be afraid. Then in the distance she saw a light which glimmered between the trees.

"There may be some people living there who can take me in for the night," thought she, and went towards the light. It was not long before she came to a house the windows of which were all lighted up. She knocked, and a rough voice from the inside, cried, "Come in." The girl stepped into the dark entrance, and knocked at the door of the room.

"Just come in," cried the voice, and when she opened the door, an old grey-haired man was sitting at the table, supporting his face with both hands, and his white beard fell down over the table almost as far as the ground. By the stove lay three animals: a hen, a cock, and a brindled cow. The girl told her story to the old man, and begged for shelter for the night. The man said,

> *"Pretty little hen,*
> *Pretty little cock,*
> *And pretty brindled cow,*
> *What say you to that?"*

"Duks," answered the animals, and that must have meant, "We are willing," for the old man said, "Here you shall have shelter and food. Go to the fire and cook us our supper."

The girl found plenty of everything in the kitchen and cooked a good supper, but never gave a thought to the animals. She carried the full dishes to the table, seated herself by the grey-haired man, and ate her fill. When she had had enough, she said, "I'm tired. Where is there a bed in which I can sleep?"

The animals replied,

> *"You have warmed yourself here,*
> *You have eaten our bread,*
> *But cared nothing for us.*
> *Go seek for your bed."*

Then the old man said, "Just go upstairs, and you will find a room with two beds. Shake them up, and put white linen on them, and I, too, will come and lie down to sleep."

The girl went up, and when she had shaken the beds and put clean sheets on, she lay down in one of them without waiting any longer for the old man. After some time, however, the grey-haired man came, took his candle, looked at the girl and shook his head. When he saw that she had fallen into a sound sleep, he opened a trap-door, and let her down into the cellar.

Late at night the woodcutter came home, and reproached his wife for leaving him hungry all day.

"It's not my fault," she replied; "the girl went out with your dinner, and must have lost herself, but she is sure to come back tomorrow."

The woodcutter arose before dawn to go into the forest, and asked that the second daughter should take him his dinner that day.

"I will take a bag of lentils," said he; "the seeds are larger than millet; the girl will see them better, and can't lose her way."

At dinner-time the girl set out with the food, but the lentils had disappeared. The birds of the forest had picked them up and had left none. The girl wandered about in the forest until night, and then she too reached the house of the old man, was told to go in, and begged for food and a bed. The man with the white beard again asked the animals,

> *"Pretty little hen,*
> *Pretty little cock,*
> *And pretty brindled cow,*
> *What say you to that?"*

The animals again replied "Duks," and everything happened just as it had happened the day before. The girl cooked a good meal, ate and drank with the old man, and did not concern herself about the animals. When she inquired about her bed they answered,

> *"You have warmed yourself here,*
> *You have eaten our bread,*
> *But cared nothing for us.*
> *Go seek for your bed."*

When she was asleep the old man came, looked at her, shook his head and let her down into the cellar.

On the third morning the woodcutter said to his wife, "Send our youngest child out with my dinner today. She has always been good and obedient, and will stay in the right path, and not run about after every wild bumblebee, as her sisters did."

The mother did not want to do it, and said, "Am I to lose my dearest child as well?"

"Have no fear," he replied. "The girl will not go astray; she is too prudent and sensible; besides I will take some peas with me, and strew them about. They are still larger than lentils, and will show her the way."

But when the girl went out with her basket on her arm, the wood-pigeons had already got all the peas in their crops, and she did not know which way to take. She was full of sorrow and never ceased to think how hungry her father would be, and how her good mother would grieve, if she did not go home.

At length when it grew dark, she saw the light and came to the house in the forest. She begged politely to be allowed to spend the night there and the man with the white beard once more asked his animals,

> *"Pretty little hen,*
> *Pretty little cock,*
> *And pretty brindled cow,*
> *What say you to that?"*

"Duks," said they.

Then the girl went to the stove where the animals were lying, and petted the cock and hen, and stroked their smooth feathers with her hand, and caressed the brindled cow between her horns, and when, in obedience to the old man's orders, she had made ready some good soup, and the bowl was placed upon the table, she said, "Am I to eat as much as I want, and the good animals to have nothing? Outside is food in plenty; I will look after them first."

So she went and brought some barley and scattered it for the cock and hen, and a whole armful of sweet-smelling hay for the cow.

"I hope you will like it, dear animals," said she, "and you shall have a refreshing draught in case you are thirsty."

Then she fetched in a bucketful of water, and the cock and hen jumped on to the edge of it and dipped their beaks in, and then held up their heads as birds do when they drink, and the brindled cow also took a hearty draught. When the animals were fed, the girl seated herself at the table by the old man, and ate what he had left. It was not long before the cock and the hen began to thrust their heads beneath their wings, and the eyes of the cow began to blink. Then said the girl, "Ought we not to go to bed?"

The animals answered "Duks,

> *"You have eaten with us,*
> *You have drunk with us,*
> *You have had kind thought for all of us.*
> *We wish you good-night."*

Then the maiden went upstairs, shook the feather-beds, and put clean sheets on them. When she had done it the old man came and lay down on one of the beds, and his white beard reached down to his feet. The girl lay down on the other, said her prayers, and fell asleep.

She slept quietly till midnight, and then there was such a noise in the house that she awoke. There was a sound of cracking and splitting in every corner, and the doors sprang open, and beat against the walls. The beams groaned as if they were being torn out of their joists. It seemed as if the staircase were falling down, and at length there was a crash as if the entire roof had fallen in. As, however, all grew quiet once more, and the girl was not hurt, she stayed quietly lying where she was, and fell asleep again. But when the brilliance of the sunshine woke her in the morning, what did she see?

She was lying in a vast hall, and everything around her shone with royal splendour. On the walls, golden flowers glowed on a ground of green silk; the bed was of ivory and the canopy of red velvet, and on a chair close by was a pair of shoes embroidered with pearls. The girl thought she must be dreaming, but three richly clad attendants came in, and asked what orders she would like to give.

"If you will go," she replied, "I will get up at once and make ready some soup for the old man, and then I will feed the pretty little hen, and the cock, and the beautiful brindled cow."

She thought the old man was up already, and looked round at his bed; he, however, was not lying in it, but a stranger. And while she was looking at him, and noticing that he was young and handsome, he awoke, sat up in bed, and said, "I am a King's son, and was bewitched by a wicked witch and made to live in this forest as an old grey-haired man. No one was allowed to be with me but my three attendants in the form of a cock, a hen, and a brindled cow. The spell was not to be broken until a girl came to us whose heart was so good that she showed herself full of love, not only towards mankind, but towards animals – and that you have done, and so at midnight, you set us free, and the old hut in the forest was changed back again into my royal palace."

The King's son ordered the three attendants to set out and fetch the father and mother of the girl to the marriage feast.

"But where are my two sisters?" inquired the maiden.

"I have locked them in the cellar, and tomorrow they shall be led into the forest to live as servants to a charcoal-burner, until they have grown kinder, so that they never let poor animals go hungry."

The Little Folks' Presents

A tailor and a goldsmith were travelling together. One evening when the sun had sunk behind the mountains, they heard the sound of distant music, which became clearer and clearer. It sounded strange, but so pleasant that they forgot all their weariness and stepped quickly onwards. The moon had already risen when they reached a hill on which they saw a crowd of little men and women who held hands to make a circle, and were whirling happily round in a dance.

They sang as they danced, and that was the music which the travellers had heard. In the midst of the dancers sat an old man who was rather taller than the rest. He wore a parti-coloured coat, and his iron-grey beard hung down over his breast. The two travellers stood full of astonishment, watching the dance. The old man made a sign that they should enter, and the little folks willingly opened their circle. The goldsmith, who had a hump, and like all hunchbacks was a brave man, stepped in; the tailor felt a little afraid at first and held back, but when he saw how merrily all was going he plucked up his courage and followed. The circle closed again directly, and the little folks went on singing and dancing with the wildest leaps.

The old man took a large knife which hung at his girdle, whetted it, and when it was sufficiently sharp he looked round at the strangers. They were terrified, but had little time for reflection, for the old man

93

seized the goldsmith and with the greatest speed shaved the hair of his head clean off, and then the same thing happened to the tailor. But their fear left them when, after he had finished his work, the old man clapped them both on the shoulder in a friendly manner, as much as to say they had behaved well to let all that be done to them willingly and without any struggle. He pointed with his finger to a heap of coals which lay at one side, and signified that they were to fill their pockets with them. Both obeyed, although they did not know what use the coals would be, and then they went on their way to seek a shelter for the night.

When they reached the valley, the clock of the neighbouring monastery struck twelve and the song ceased. In a moment all had vanished, and the hill lay in solitude in the moonlight.

The two travellers found an inn, and covered themselves up on their straw beds with their coats, but in their weariness forgot to take the coals out of them. A heavy weight on their limbs awakened them earlier than usual. They felt in their pockets, and could not believe their eyes when they saw that they were not filled with coals, but with pure gold. Happily, too, the hair of their heads and beards was there again as thick as ever.

They had now become rich, but the goldsmith, who, because he was greedy, had filled his pockets better, was twice as rich as the tailor. A greedy man, even if he has much, always wants more, so the goldsmith proposed to the tailor that they should stay another day and go out again that evening in order to bring back still greater treasures from the old man on the hill.

The tailor refused, and said, "I have enough and am content. Now I shall be my own master, and marry my sweetheart, and be a happy man." But he stayed another day to please the goldsmith.

In the evening the goldsmith hung a couple of bags over his shoulders so that he could stow away a great deal, and took the road to the hill. He found the little folks at their singing and dancing, and the old man again shaved him clean and signed to him to take some coal away with him. He was not slow about stuffing as much into his bags as would go, came back to the inn quite delighted, and covered himself over with his coat.

"Even if the gold does weigh heavily," said he, "I will gladly bear that."

At last he fell asleep with the sweet anticipation of waking an enormously rich man. When he woke next morning he leapt up to examine his pockets. How amazed he was when he drew nothing out of them but black coals.

"But I still have the gold I got the night before," thought he, and went and brought it out, but it too had turned back to coal! He smote his forehead with his dusty black hand, and then he felt that his whole head was bald and smooth, as was also the place where his beard should have been. Then he knew he had been punished for greediness, and began to weep aloud.

The good tailor, who was wakened by this, comforted the unhappy fellow as best he could, and said, "You have been my comrade on my travels, you shall stay with me and share my wealth."

And he kept his word.

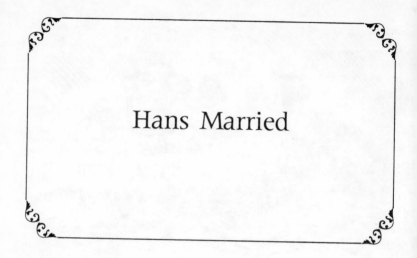

Hans Married

There was once upon a time a young peasant named Hans, whose uncle wanted to find him a rich wife. So he sat Hans behind the stove, and had it made very hot. Then he fetched a pot of milk and plenty of white bread, put a bright newly-coined farthing into his hand, and said, "Hans, hold that farthing fast, crumble the white bread into the milk, stay where you are, and do not stir from that spot till I come back."

"Yes," said Hans, "I'll do all that."

Then the matchmaker put on a pair of old patched trousers, went to a rich peasant's daughter in the next village, and said, "Will you marry my nephew Hans? You will get an honest and sensible man who will suit you."

Her covetous father asked, "What about his means? Does he live well?"

"Dear friend," replied the matchmaker, "my young nephew has a snug berth, a nice bit of money in hand, and lives very well; besides he has quite as many patches as I have" (and as he spoke, he slapped the patches on his trousers, but in that district small pieces of land were called patches also). "If you'll be good enough to go home with me, you'll see at once that all is as I've said."

The girl's father did not want to lose this good opportunity, and

said, "If that's the case, I have nothing further to say against the marriage."

So the wedding was celebrated on the appointed day, and when the young wife went out of doors to see the bridegroom's property, Hans took off his Sunday coat and put on his patched smock and said, "I might spoil my good coat." Then together they went out and wherever a boundary line came in sight, or fields and meadows were divided from each other, Hans pointed with his finger and then slapped either a large or a small patch on his smock and said, "That patch is mine, and that too, my dearest, just look at it," meaning thereby that his wife should not stare at other people's acres, but look at his garment, which was his own.

The Twelve Huntsmen

There was once a King's son who was betrothed to a maiden whom he loved very much. And when he was sitting beside her and very happy, news came that his father lay sick, and desired to see him once again before his end.

Then he said to his beloved, "I must go now and leave you, but I give you this ring as a remembrance of me. When I am King, I will return and fetch you."

So he rode away, and when he reached his father the King was dangerously ill, and near his death. He said to him, "Dear son, I wished to see you once again before my end. Promise me to marry as I wish," and he named a certain King's daughter who was to be his wife. The son was in such trouble that he did not think what he was doing, and said, "Yes, dear father, your will shall be done," and thereupon the King shut his eyes, and died.

When therefore the son had been proclaimed King, and the time of mourning was over, he was forced to keep the promise given to his father. He asked for the King's daughter in marriage, and she was promised to him. His first betrothed heard of this, and fretted so much about his faithlessness that she nearly died.

Then her father said to her, "Dearest child, why are you so sad? I'll give you whatever you desire."

She thought for a moment and said, "Dear father, I wish for eleven girls exactly like myself in face, figure, and size."

The father said, "If it be possible, your wish shall be granted," and he caused a search to be made in his whole kingdom, until eleven maidens were found who exactly resembled his daughter.

The King's daughter had twelve suits of huntsmen's clothes made, all alike, and the eleven maidens had to put on the huntsmen's clothes, and she herself put on the twelfth suit. Then she took leave of her father, and rode away with them to the court of her former betrothed, whom she loved so dearly. She asked if he required any huntsmen, and if he would take all of them into his service. The King looked at her and did not know her, but as they were such handsome fellows, he said, "Yes," and that he would willingly take them. And now they were the King's twelve huntsmen.

The King, however, had a lion which was a wondrous animal, for he knew all hidden and secret things. One evening he said to the King, "You fancy you have twelve huntsmen there, don't you?"

"Yes," said the King.

The lion continued, "You are mistaken; they are twelve girls."

The King said, "That cannot be true! How will you prove it?"

"Oh, just have some peas strewn in your ante-chamber," answered the lion, "and then you'll soon see. Men have a firm step, and when they walk over peas none of them stir, but girls trip and skip, and the peas roll about."

The King was well pleased with the counsel, and caused the peas to be strewn.

There was, however, a servant of the King's who admired the huntsmen, and when he heard that they were going to be put to this test he went to them and repeated everything, and said, "The lion wants to make the King believe that you are girls."

Then the King's daughter thanked him, and said to her maidens, "Do your best to tread firmly on the peas."

Next morning when the King summoned the twelve huntsmen, they came into the ante-chamber where the peas were lying, and stepped so firmly on them that not one of the peas either rolled or stirred.

Then they went away again, and the King said to the lion, "You lied to me; they walk just like men."

The lion said, "They were warned and so they walked like men. Just have twelve spinning-wheels brought into the ante-chamber tomorrow, and they will go to them and be pleased with them, as no man would be." The King liked the advice, and had the spinning-wheels placed in the ante-chamber.

But again the kind servant went to the huntsmen and disclosed the plan. When they were alone the King's daughter said to her eleven girls, "Control yourselves, and do not even glance at the spinning-wheels."

Next morning when the King had his twelve huntsmen summoned, they went through the ante-chamber, and never once looked at the spinning-wheels. Then the King again said to the lion, "You have deceived me. They *are* men. They never looked at the spinning-wheels."

The lion replied, "They knew that they were going to be put to the test, and restrained themselves."

The King, however, would no longer believe the lion.

The twelve huntsmen always accompanied the King when he went hunting, and he grew more and more fond of them. Now it chanced that once when they were out hunting, news came that the King's betrothed was approaching. When the true bride heard this, it distressed her so much that she fell fainting to the ground. The King thought something had happened to his favourite huntsman, ran up to help him, and drew off his glove. He saw the ring which he had given to his first betrothed, and when he looked in her face he recognized her.

Then his heart was so touched that he kissed her, and when she opened her eyes he said, "You are mine, and I am yours, and no one in the world can alter that."

He sent a messenger to the other bride, and entreated her to return to her own kingdom, for he had a wife already, and a man who had just found an old dish did not require a new one. Thereupon the wedding was celebrated, and the lion was again taken into favour, because after all he had told the truth.

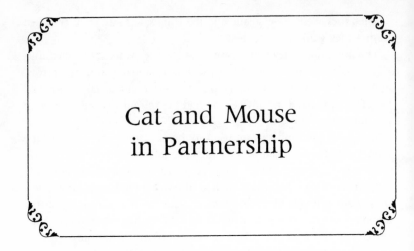

Cat and Mouse
in Partnership

A cat once made the acquaintance of a mouse, and said so much about the love and friendship she felt for her, that at length the mouse agreed that they should keep house together.

"But we must make provision for winter, or else we shall go hungry," said the cat, "and you, little mouse, cannot venture everywhere, or you will be caught in a trap someday."

The good advice was followed, and a pot of fat was bought, but they did not know where to put it. At length, after much consideration, the cat said, "I know no place where it will be better stored than in the church, for no one dares take anything away from there. We'll set it beneath the altar, and not touch it until we are really in need of it."

So the pot was placed in safety, but it was not long before the cat had a great longing for it, and said to the mouse, "Little mouse, my cousin has brought a son into the world, and has asked me to be godmother; he is white with brown spots, and I am to hold him at the christening. Let me go out today, and you look after the house by yourself."

"Yes," answered the mouse, "by all means go, and if you get anything very good, think of me. I'd like a drop of sweet red christening wine too."

All this, however, was untrue; the cat had no cousin, and had not been asked to be godmother. She went straight to the church, stole to

the pot of fat, began to lick at it, and licked the top of the fat off. Then she took a walk over the roofs of the town, ready to pounce on any bird, and stretched herself in the sun, and licked her lips whenever she thought of the pot of fat. Not until evening did she return home.

"Well, here you are again," said the mouse. "No doubt you have had a merry day."

"All went well," answered the cat.

"What name did they give the child?"

"Top-off!" said the cat quite coolly.

"Top-off!" cried the mouse. "That is a very odd and uncommon name. Is it a usual one in your family?"

"What does it matter?" said the cat. "It is no worse than Crumb-stealer, as your godchildren are called."

Before long the cat was seized by another fit of longing. She said to the mouse, "Do me a favour, and once more manage the house for a day. I am again asked to be godmother, and, as the child has a white ring round its neck, I can't refuse."

The good mouse consented, but the cat crept behind the town walls to the church and devoured half the pot of fat.

"Nothing tastes better than what one eats by oneself," said she.

When she went home the mouse inquired, "And what was this child christened?"

"Half-gone," answered the cat.

"Half-gone! What are you saying? I never heard the name in my life. I'll wager anything it is not in the calendar!"

The cat's mouth soon began to water for some more licking.

"All good things go in threes," said she. "I am asked to stand godmother again. The child is quite black, only it has white paws, but not another white hair on its whole body. This only happens once every few years, so you will let me go, won't you?"

"Top-off! Half-gone!" answered the mouse. "They are such odd names, they make me very thoughtful."

"You sit at home," said the cat, "in your dark grey fur coat and long tail, your head filled with fancies. That's because you never go out in the daytime."

During the cat's absence the mouse cleaned the house, and put it in order, but meanwhile the greedy cat entirely emptied the pot of fat.

"When everything is eaten up one has some peace," said she to herself, and well filled and plump she did not return home till night. The mouse at once asked what name had been given to the third child.

"It will please you no more than the others," said the cat. "He is called All-gone."

"All-gone!" cried the mouse. "That is the most suspicious name of all! I have never seen it in print. All-gone; what can that mean?" And she shook her head, curled herself up, and lay down to sleep.

From this time forth no one invited the cat to be godmother, but when the winter had come and there was no longer anything to be found outside, the mouse thought of their store, and said, "Come, cat,
104

we will go to our pot of fat which we have saved up for ourselves – we shall enjoy that."

"Yes," answered the cat, "you'll enjoy it as much as you would enjoy putting that dainty tongue of yours out of the window."

They set out on their way, but when they arrived, the pot of fat certainly was still in its place, but it was empty.

"Alas!" said the mouse. "Now I see what has happened; now it comes to light! You are a true friend! You ate it all when you were standing godmother. First top-off, then half-gone, then –"

"Will you hold your tongue!" cried the cat. "One word more, and I will eat you too."

"All-gone" was already on the poor mouse's lips; scarcely had she spoken it before the cat sprang on her, seized her, and gobbled her up. Alas, that is the way of the world.

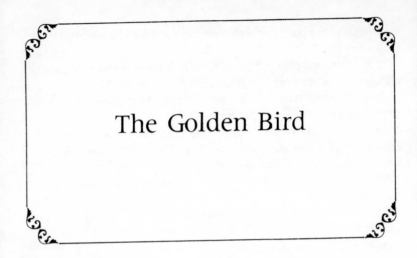

The Golden Bird

Long, long ago there was a king, who had behind his palace a beautiful pleasure-garden, and there a tree bore golden apples. When the apples were getting ripe they were counted, but next morning one was missing. So the King ordered a watch to be kept every night beneath the tree.

The king had three sons, the eldest of whom he sent, as soon as night came, into the garden; but at midnight he could not keep himself from sleeping, and next morning another apple was gone.

The following night the second son had to keep watch. It fared no better with him: as soon as twelve o'clock had struck he fell asleep, and in the morning an apple was gone.

Now it came to the turn of the third son to watch. He was quite willing, but the King had not much trust in him, and thought he would be of less use even than his brothers; but at last he let him go. The youth lay down beneath the tree, but kept awake, and did not let sleep master him.

When it struck twelve, something rustled through the air, and in the moonlight he saw a bird coming, its feathers all shining with gold. The bird alighted on the tree, and had just plucked off an apple when the youth shot an arrow at it. The bird flew off, but the arrow had struck its plumage, and one of its golden feathers fell down. The youth picked it up, and the next morning took it to the King and told him what he had seen in the night.

The King called his council together, and everyone declared that a feather like this was worth more than the whole kingdom.

"If the feather is so precious," declared the King, "one alone will not do for me; I must and will have the whole bird!"

The eldest son set out; he trusted to his cleverness, and thought that he would easily find the Golden Bird. When he had gone some distance he saw a Fox sitting at the edge of a wood, so he cocked his gun and took aim at him.

The Fox cried, "Do not shoot me, and in return I will give you some good counsel. You are on the way to the Golden Bird. This evening you will come to a village in which stand two inns opposite to one another. One of them is lighted up brightly, and all will be merry there, but do not go into it; go rather into the other, even though it seems a poor one."

"How can such a silly beast give wise advice?" thought the prince, and he pulled the trigger. But he missed the Fox, who turned and ran quickly into the wood.

So he went on his way, and by evening came to the village where the two inns were. In one they were singing and dancing; the other had a poor, miserable look.

"I should be a fool indeed," he thought, "if I were to go into the shabby tavern, and pass by the good one." So he went into the cheerful one, lived there in rioting and revelling, and forgot the bird and his father, and all good counsels.

When some time had passed, and the eldest son for month after month did not return home, the second set out to find the Golden Bird. The Fox met him as he had met the eldest, and gave him the good advice of which he took no heed. He came to the two inns, and his brother was standing at the window of the one from which came the sound of music, and called out to him. He could not resist, but went inside and lived only for pleasure.

Again some time passed, and then the King's youngest son wanted to set off and try his luck, but his father would not allow it.

"It is no use," said he; "he will be even less able to find the Golden

Bird than his brothers, and if a mishap were to befall him he will not know how to help himself. He is not very bright."

But at last, as he had no peace, he let him go.

Again the Fox was sitting outside the wood, and begged for his life, and offered his good advice. The youth was good-natured, and said, "Don't worry, little Fox, I will do you no harm."

"You won't regret it," answered the Fox; "and so that you may go faster, get up behind my tail."

Scarcely had he seated himself than the Fox began to run, and away they went over stock and stone till his hair whistled in the wind. When they came to the village the prince got off; he followed the good advice, and without looking round turned into the little inn, where he spent the night quietly.

The next morning, as soon as he got into the open country, there sat the Fox who said, "I'll now tell you what you have to do next. Go straight on till you come to a castle, in front of which a whole regiment of soldiers is lying. Don't trouble yourself about them, for they will all be asleep and snoring. Go through the midst of them straight into the castle, through all the rooms, till at last you'll come to a chamber where a Golden Bird is hanging in a wooden cage. Close by there stands an empty gold cage for show, but beware of taking the bird out of the wooden cage and putting it into the gold one, or it may go badly with you."

With these words the Fox again stretched out his tail, and the prince seated himself upon it, and away they went over stock and stone till his hair whistled in the wind.

When he came to the castle he found everything as the Fox had said. The prince went into the chamber where the Golden Bird was shut up in a wooden cage, while a golden one stood hard by; and three golden apples lay about the room.

"But," thought the prince, "it would be absurd to leave the beautiful bird in the common and ugly cage," so he opened the door, laid hold of it, and put it into the golden cage.

The bird uttered a shrill cry. The soldiers awoke, rushed in, and took the prince off to prison. The next morning he was taken before a court of justice, and, as he confessed everything, was sentenced to death.

The King, however, said he would grant him his life on one condition – namely, if he brought him the Golden Horse which ran faster than the wind. In addition he would receive as a reward the Golden Bird.

The prince set off, but he sighed and was sorrowful, for how was he to find the Golden Horse? But all at once he saw his old friend the Fox sitting on the road.

"You now see," said the Fox, "what happened because you did not heed me. However, be of good courage. I'll tell you how to get to the Golden Horse. Go straight on, and you will come to a castle. In the stable stands the horse. The grooms will be lying in front of the stable; but they will be asleep and snoring, and you can quietly lead out the Golden Horse. But of one thing you must take heed: put on him the common saddle of wood and leather, and not the golden one, which hangs close by, else it will go ill with you."

Then the Fox stretched out his tail, the prince seated himself upon it, and away they went over stock and stone until his hair whistled in the wind.

Everything happened just as the Fox had said. The prince came to the stable in which the Golden Horse was standing, but just as he was going to put the common saddle upon him, he thought, "It will be an insult to such a beautiful beast not to give him the good saddle which belongs to him by right."

Scarcely had the golden saddle touched the horse than he began to neigh loudly. The grooms awoke, seized the youth, and threw him into prison. The next morning he was sentenced by the court to death; but the King promised to grant him his life, and the Golden Horse as well, if he could bring back the beautiful princess from the Golden Castle.

With a heavy heart the youth set out; yet luckily for him he soon found the trusty Fox.

"I ought by rights to leave you to your ill-luck," said the Fox, "but I pity you, and will help you once more out of your trouble. This road takes you straight to the Golden Castle; you will reach it by eventide. At night when everything is quiet the beautiful princess goes to the bath-house to bathe. When she enters it, run up to her and give her a kiss, then she will follow you, and you can take her away with you; only do not allow her to take leave of her parents first, or it will go ill with you."

Then the Fox stretched out his tail, the prince seated himself upon it, and away they went, over stock and stone, till his hair whistled in the wind.

When he reached the Golden Castle it was just as the Fox had said. He waited until midnight, when everything lay in deep sleep, and the beautiful princess was going to the bath-house. Then he sprang out and gave her a kiss. She said that she would like to go with him, but she asked him pitifully, and with tears, to allow her first to take leave of her parents. At first he withstood her prayer, but when she wept more and more, and fell at his feet, he at last gave in. But no sooner had the maiden reached the bedside of her father than he and all the rest in the castle awoke, and the youth was seized and put into prison.

The next morning the King said to him, "Your life is forfeited, and you can only find mercy if you take away the hill which stands in front of my windows, and prevents my seeing beyond it; and you must finish it all within eight days. If you do that you shall have my daughter as your reward."

The prince began, and dug and shovelled without leaving off, but when after seven days he saw how little he had done, he was very sad

and gave up all hope. But on the evening of the seventh day the Fox appeared and said, "You don't deserve any more help from me; but just lie down and go to sleep, and I'll do the work for you."

The next morning when he awoke and looked out of the window the hill had gone. The youth ran, full of joy, to the King, and told him that the task was fulfilled, and whether he liked it or not he must keep his word and give him his daughter. So the prince and the maiden set forth together, and it was not long before the trusty Fox came up with them.

"You have certainly got what is best," said he, "but the Golden Horse also belongs to the maiden of the Golden Castle."

"How shall I get it?" asked the prince.

"That I'll tell you," answered the Fox. "First take the beautiful maiden to the King who sent you to the Golden Castle. There will be unheard-of rejoicing; they will gladly give you the Golden Horse, and will bring it out to you. Mount it as soon as possible, and offer your hand to all in farewell; last of all to the beautiful maiden. And as soon as you have taken her hand swing her up on the horse, and gallop away, and no one will be able to bring you back, for the horse runs faster than the wind."

All this was successfully done, and the prince carried off the beautiful princess on the Golden Horse.

The Fox soon joined them, and he said to the prince, "Now I will help you to get the Golden Bird. When you come near to the castle where the Golden Bird is to be found, let the maiden get down, and I will take her into my care. Then ride with the Golden Horse into the castle yard; there will be great rejoicing at sight of it, and they will bring out the Golden Bird for you. As soon as you have the cage in your hand gallop back to us, and take the maiden away again."

When the plan had succeeded, and the prince was about to ride home with his treasures, the Fox said, "Now you must reward me for my help."

"What do you require for it?" asked the prince.

"When you get into the wood yonder, shoot me dead, and chop off my head and feet."

"That would be fine gratitude," said the prince. "I cannot possibly do that for you."

The Fox said, "If you won't do it I must leave you, but before I go away I'll give you a piece of good advice. Be careful about two things. Buy no gallows' meat, and do not sit on the edge of any well." And then he ran into the wood.

The prince thought, "That is a strange beast, with strange whims. Who would want to buy gallows' meat? And the desire to sit at the edge of a well has never yet seized me."

He rode on with the beautiful maiden, and his road took him again through the village in which his brothers had remained. There was a great stir and noise, and when he asked what was going on, he was told that two men were going to be hanged. As he came nearer to the place he saw that they were his two brothers, who had been playing all kinds of wicked pranks, and had squandered all their wealth. He asked whether they could not be set free.

"If you will pay for them," answered the people. "But why should you waste your money on wicked men, and buy their freedom?"

He did not think twice about it, but paid for them, and when they were set free they all went on their way together.

They came to the wood where the Fox had first met them, and as it was cool and pleasant within it, while the sun shone hotly outside, the two brothers said, "Let us rest a little by the well, and eat and drink."

He agreed, and while they were talking he forgot the warning and sat down upon the edge of the well without suspecting foul play. But the two brothers threw him backwards into the well, took the maiden, the Horse and the Bird, and went home to their father.

"Here we bring you not only the Golden Bird," said they. "We have won the Golden Horse also, and the maiden from the Golden Castle."

Then was there great joy; but the Horse would not eat, the Bird would not sing, and the maiden sat and wept.

But the youngest brother was not dead. By good fortune the well was dry, and he fell upon soft moss without being hurt, but he could not get out again. Even in this strait the faithful Fox did not leave him: he came and leapt down to him, and upbraided him for having forgotten his advice.

"But even so I can't leave you to your fate," he said. "I will help you up again into daylight."

He bade him grasp his tail and keep tight hold of it; and then he pulled him up.

"You are not out of all danger yet," said the Fox. "Your brothers were not sure of your death, and have surrounded the wood with watchers who will kill you if they see you."

But a poor man was sitting by the road. The prince changed clothes with him, and in this way he got to the King's palace.

No one knew him, but the Bird began to sing, the Horse began to eat, and the beautiful maiden left off weeping. The King, astonished, asked, "What does this mean?"

Then the maiden said, "I do not know, but I have been so sad and now I am so happy! I feel as if my true bridegroom had come." She told him all that had happened, although the other brothers had threatened her with death if she were to betray them.

The King commanded that all people who were in his castle should be brought before him; and among them came the prince in his ragged clothes; but the maiden knew him at once and fell upon his neck. The wicked brothers were seized and put to death, but the prince married the beautiful maiden and was proclaimed heir to the King.

But how did it fare with the poor Fox? Long afterwards the prince was once again walking in the wood, when the Fox met him and said, "You have everything now that you can wish for, but there is never an end to my misery, and yet it is in your power to free me," and again he asked him with tears to shoot him dead and to chop off his head and feet. So the prince did it. At once the Fox was changed into a man; and was no other than the brother of the beautiful princess, who at last was freed from the evil spell which had been laid upon him. And now nothing more was wanting to their happiness as long as they lived.

The Rogue
and his Master

A certain man named John wanted his son to learn some trade, and he went into the church to ask the priest which would be the best. Just then the Clerk who was standing near the altar cried out, "A thief, a rogue!"

At these words the man went away and told his son he must learn to be a rogue for so the Priest had said. So they set out and asked one man after another whether he was a rogue. At the end of the day they came to a large forest, and there they found a little hut with an old woman in it.

John says, "Do you know any man who is good at thieving?"

"You can learn that here quite well," says the old woman; "my son is a master of it."

So John asks the son if he can teach *his* son thieving really well. The master-thief says, "I'll teach him well. Come back when a year is over, and then if you can recognize your son I'll take no payment at all for teaching him; but if you don't know him, you must give me two hundred thalers."

The father goes home and the son learns witchcraft and thieving thoroughly. When the year is out, the father is anxious to know how he can be sure to recognize his son. As he walks along, frowning with

worry, he meets a little dwarf, who says, "Man, what ails you? You seem to be in trouble."

"Oh," says John, "a year ago I placed my son with a master-thief who told me I was to come back when the year was out, and that if I then didn't know my son when I saw him, I was to pay two hundred thalers, but if I did know him I was to pay nothing; and now I'm afraid of not knowing him and where am I to find the money?"

The dwarf tells him to take a small basket of bread, and to stand beneath the chimney. "There on the cross-beam is a basket, out of which a little bird is peeping. That's your son."

John goes thither, and throws a basketful of black bread in front of the basket, and the little bird peeps out.

"Hello, is that you, my son?" says the father, and the son is delighted to see him.

But the master-thief says angrily, "A witch must have helped you! How else could you have known your son?"

"Father, let's go," says the youth.

Then the father and son set out homeward. On the way a carriage comes driving by. The son says to his father, "I will change myself into a large greyhound, and then you can sell me and earn a great deal of money."

Then the gentleman calls from the carriage, "My man, will you sell your dog?"

"Yes," says the father.

"How much do you want for it?"

"Thirty thalers."

"Eh, man, that's a great deal, but as it's such a very fine dog I'll have it."

The gentleman takes it into his carriage, but when they have driven a little further the dog springs out of the carriage through the window, and goes back to his father, and is no longer a greyhound.

They go home together. Next day there is a fair in the neighbouring town, so the youth says to his father, "I'll change myself into a beautiful horse, and you can sell me; but when you have sold me, you must take off my bridle, or I can't become a man again."

The father goes with the horse to the fair, and the master-thief comes and buys the horse for a hundred thalers, but the father forgets to take off the bridle. So the man goes home with the horse, and puts it in the stable. When the maidservant crosses the threshold, the horse says, "Take off my bridle, take off my bridle."

She stops in astonishment, and says, "What, can you speak?"

She takes the bridle off, and the horse becomes a sparrow, and flies out at the door, and the master-thief becomes a sparrow also, and flies after him. Then they meet and cast lots, but the master loses, and slips into the water and is a fish. Then the youth too becomes a fish and they cast lots again, and the master loses. So the master changes himself into a cock, and the youth becomes a fox, and bites the master's head off, and he died and has remained dead to this day.

The Wolf
and the
Seven Little Kids

There was once upon a time an old goat who had seven kids, and loved them all dearly. One day she wanted to go into the forest to fetch some food. So she called all seven to her and said, "Dear children, I have to go into the forest. Be on your guard against the wolf; if he comes in, he'll devour you – skin, hair and all. The wretch often disguises himself; but you'll know him at once by his rough voice and his black feet."

The kids said, "Dear mother, we'll take good care of ourselves; don't worry about us."

The old mother goat bleated, and went on her way with an easy mind.

It was not long before someone knocked on the house-door and cried, "Open the door, dear children. Your mother is here, and has brought something back with her for each of you."

But the little kids knew by the rough voice that it was the wolf. "We won't open the door," cried they; "you are not our mother. She has a soft, pleasant voice but your voice is rough; you are the wolf!"

Then the wolf went away to a shopkeeper and bought himself a great lump of chalk, ate this and made his voice soft with it. Then he came back, knocked on the door of the house, and cried, "Open the

118

door, dear children. Your mother is here and has brought something back with her for each of you."

But the wolf laid his black paws against the window, and the children saw them and cried, "We won't open the door; our mother hasn't got black feet; you are the wolf!"

Then the wolf ran to a baker and said, "I have hurt my feet, rub some dough over them for me."

When the baker had rubbed his feet with dough, the wolf ran to the miller and said, "Sprinkle some white flour over my feet for me."

The miller thought to himself, "The wolf wants to deceive someone," and refused; but the wolf said, "If you won't do it, I'll devour you." Then the miller was afraid, and made his paws white for him. Yes, men are like that!

So now the wicked wolf went for the third time to the house-door, knocked at it, and said, "Open the door, dear children. Your mother is here, and has brought something back with her for each of you."

The little kids cried, "First show us your paws so that we may know if you are our mother."

Then he put his paws in through the window, and when the kids saw that they were white, they believed that all he said was true, and opened the door. Who should come in but the wolf! They were terrified and tried to hide themselves. One sprang under the table, the second into the bed, the third into the stove, the fourth into the kitchen, the fifth into the cupboard, the sixth under the washing-bowl, and the seventh into the clock-case. But the wolf found them, and made short work of six of them: one after the other he swallowed them. The youngest in the clock-case was the only one he did not find.

When the wolf had satisfied his appetite he took himself off, laid himself down under a tree in the green meadow outside, and went to sleep.

Soon afterwards the old goat came home again from the forest. Oh, what a sight met her eyes! The house-door stood wide open. The table, chairs and benches were overturned, the washing-bowl lay broken in pieces, and the quilts and pillows were pulled off the bed. She looked everywhere for her children, but they were nowhere to be found. She called them one after the other by name, but no one answered. At last, when she came to the youngest, a soft voice cried, "Dear mother, I am in the clock-case."

She took the kid out, and he told her how the wolf had come and had eaten all the others. You may imagine how she wept over her poor children.

At length in her grief she went out, and the youngest kid ran with her. When they came to the meadow, there lay the wolf by the tree snoring so loudly that the branches shook. She looked at him from every side and saw that something was moving and struggling in his gorged body.

"Ah, heavens," she cried, "is it possible that my poor children whom he has swallowed down for his supper can still be alive ?"

She sent the kid running home to fetch scissors and a needle and thread. Then the goat cut open the monster's stomach, and hardly had she made one cut when one little kid thrust its head out, and when she had cut further, all six sprang out one after another, and were all still alive, and had suffered no injury whatever, for in his greed the monster had swallowed them down whole. You can guess how happy their mother was – and the kids embraced her and skipped about like a tailor at his wedding.

At last she said, "Now go and look for some big stones, and we will fill the wicked beast's stomach with them while he is still asleep."

The seven kids dragged the stones to her as fast as they could, and stuffed as many of them into his stomach as it would hold. The mother sewed him up again in haste, so that he was not aware of anything and never once stirred.

When the wolf at length had had his sleep out, he got on his legs, and as the stones in his stomach made him very thirsty, he wanted to go to the well to drink. But when he began to walk the stones in his stomach knocked against each other and rattled. Then he cried,

> *"What rumbles and tumbles*
> *Against my poor bones ?*
> *Not little kids, I think,*
> *But only big stones."*

And when he got to the well and stooped over the water to drink, the heavy stones made him fall in and he drowned miserably.

When the seven kids saw what had happened, they came running up and cried aloud, "The wolf is dead! The wolf is dead!" and danced for joy round the well with their mother.

Brother and Sister

Little brother took his little sister by the hand and said, "Since our mother died we have had no happiness; our stepmother beats us every day, and if we come near her she kicks us away with her foot. Our meals are the hard crusts of bread that are left over; and the little dog under the table is better off, for she often throws it a tasty morsel. Heaven have pity on us! If our mother only knew! Come, we'll go together into the wide world."

They walked the whole day over meadows, fields, and stony places; and when it rained the little sister said, "Heaven and our hearts are weeping together." In the evening they came to a forest, and they were so weary with sorrow and hunger and the long walk, that they lay down in a hollow tree and fell asleep.

The next day when they awoke, the sun was already high in the sky, and shone down hot into the tree. Then the brother said, "Sister, I am thirsty; if I could find a little brook I'd go and have a drink; I think I hear one running." The brother got up and took his little sister by the hand, and they set off to find the brook.

But the wicked stepmother was a witch, and had seen how the two children had gone away, and had crept after them secretly, as witches do, and had bewitched all the brooks in the forest. So when they found a little brook sparkling over the stones, the brother was going to drink out of it, but his sister heard how it said as it ran, "Who drinks of me will be a tiger; who drinks of me will be a tiger."

Then the sister cried, "Pray, dear brother, don't drink, or you will become a wild beast, and tear me to pieces."

Her brother did not drink, although he was so thirsty, but said, "I'll wait for the next spring."

When they came to the next brook the sister heard this one also say, "Who drinks of me will be a wolf; who drinks of me will be a wolf."

Then the sister cried, "Pray, dear brother, do not drink, or you will become a wolf and devour me."

Her brother did not drink, and said, "I'll wait until we come to the next spring, but then I must drink, say what you like; for my thirst is too great."

And when they came to the third brook the sister heard how it said, "Who drinks of me will be a roebuck; who drinks of me will be a roebuck."

The sister said, "Oh, I pray you, dear brother, do not drink, or you will become a roebuck and run away from me." But her brother knelt down at once by the brook, and drank some of the water, and as soon as the first drops touched his lips, there he lay: a young roebuck.

The sister wept over her poor bewitched brother, and the little roe wept also, and sat sorrowfully near to her. But at last the girl said, "Stop crying, dear little roe, for I'll never, never leave you." Then she untied her golden garter and put it round the roebuck's neck, and she plucked rushes, and wove them into a soft cord. With this she tied the little animal and led it deeper and deeper into the forest.

When they had gone a very long way they came at last to a little house, and the girl looked in; and as it was empty, she thought, "We can stay and live here." Then she looked for leaves and moss to make a soft bed for the roe; and every morning she went out and gathered roots and berries and nuts for herself, and brought tender grass for the roe, who ate out of her hand, and played happily round about her. In the evening, when the sister was tired, and had said her prayers, she laid her head upon the roebuck's back; that was her pillow, and she

slept softly on it. And if only her brother had had his human form it would have been a delightful life.

For some time they were alone like this in the wilderness. But it happened that the king of the country held a great hunt in the forest. Then the blasts of the horns, the barking of dogs, and the merry shouts of the huntsmen rang through the trees, and the roebuck heard all, and was only too anxious to be there.

"Oh," said he to his sister, "let me be off to the hunt; I cannot bear it any longer"; and he begged so much that at last she agreed.

"But," said she, "come back to me in the evening; I must shut my door for fear of the rough huntsmen, so knock and say 'Little sister, let me in!' that I may know you; and if you do not say that, I shall not open the door." Then the young roebuck sprang away, happy and merry to be in the open air.

The King and the huntsmen saw the pretty creature, and started after him, but they could not catch him. When they thought that they surely had him, away he sprang through the bushes and could not be seen. When it was dark he ran to the cottage, knocked, and said, "Little sister, let me in." Then the door was opened for him, and he jumped in, and slept the whole night through on his soft bed.

The next day the hunt went on afresh, and when the roebuck again heard the bugle-horn, and the "Tally ho!" of the huntsmen, he had no peace, but said, "Sister, let me out, I must be off."

His sister opened the door for him, and said, "But you must be here again in the evening and say your password."

When the King and his huntsmen again saw the young roebuck with the golden collar, they chased him, but he was too quick and nimble for them. This went on for the whole day, but at last by the evening the huntsmen had surrounded him, and one of them wounded him a little in the foot, so that he limped and ran slowly. Then a hunter crept after him to the cottage and heard how he said, "Little sister, let me in," and saw that the door was opened for him, and was shut again at once. The huntsman went to the King and told him what he had seen and heard. Then the King said, "Tomorrow we will hunt once more."

The little sister, however, was dreadfully frightened when she saw that her fawn was hurt. She washed the blood off him, laid herbs on the wound, and said, "Go to your bed, dear roe, that you may get well again."

The wound was so slight that next morning the roebuck did not feel it any more. And when he again heard the huntsmen outside, he said, "I cannot bear it, I must be there."

The sister cried and said, "This time they will kill you, and here am I alone in the forest, forsaken by all the world. I will not let you out."

"Then you will have me die of grief," answered the roe. "When I hear the bugle-horns I feel as if I must jump out of my skin."

Then his sister was forced to open the door for him with a heavy heart, and the roebuck, full of health and joy, bounded into the forest. When the King saw him, he said to his huntsmen, "Now chase him all day long till nightfall, but take care that no one does him any harm."

As soon as the sun had set, the King said to the huntsmen, "Now come and show me the cottage in the wood"; and when he was at the door, he knocked and called out, "Little sister, let me in!"

Then the door opened, and there stood a maiden more lovely than any the King had ever seen. She was frightened when she saw, not her little roe, but a man who wore a golden crown upon his head. But the King looked kindly at her, stretched out his hand, and said, "Will you go with me to my palace and be my dear wife?"

"Yes, indeed," answered the maiden. "But the little roe must go with me. I cannot leave him."

The King said, "It shall stay with you as long as you live, and want nothing." Just then the roe came running in, and the sister again tied him with the cord of rushes, took it in her hand, and went with the King from the cottage.

The King took the lovely maiden upon his horse and rode to his palace, where the wedding was held with great pomp. She was now the Queen, and they lived for a long time happily together. The roebuck was tended and cherished, and ran about in the palace garden.

But the wicked stepmother, whose unkindness had driven the children out into the world, thought all the time that the sister had been torn to pieces by the wild beasts in the wood, and that the brother had been shot for a roebuck by the huntsmen. Now when she heard that they were so happy, and so well off, envy and hatred rose in her heart and left her no peace, and she thought of nothing but how she could bring them again to misfortune. Her own daughter, who was as ugly as night, and had only one eye, grumbled and said, "A Queen! That ought to have been my luck."

"Just be patient," said her mother, "I'll know what to do when the time comes."

A year went by, and the Queen had a pretty little boy. It happened that the king went out hunting; so the wicked stepmother, who was a witch, took the form of the chambermaid, went into the room where the Queen lay, and said to her, "Come, the bath is ready. It will do you good, and give you fresh strength; make haste before it gets cold."

The daughter also was close by; so they carried the weakly Queen into the bathroom, and put her into the bath; then they shut the door and ran away. But in the bathroom they had made a fire of such deadly heat that the beautiful young Queen was soon suffocated.

When this was done the old woman took her daughter, put a nightcap on her head, and laid her in bed in place of the Queen. She gave her too the shape and look of the Queen, only she could not make good the lost eye. But in order that the King might not see it, she was to lie on the side on which she had no eye.

In the evening when he came home and heard that he had a son the King was very happy, and hurried to the bed of his dear wife to see how she was. But the stepmother quickly called out, "Be sure to leave the curtains closed; the Queen ought not to see the light yet, and must have rest."

The King went away, and did not find out that a false Queen was lying in the bed.

But at midnight, when all others slept, the nurse, who was sitting in the nursery by the cradle, saw the door open and the true Queen walk in. She took the child out of the cradle, laid it on her arm, and nursed it. Then she shook up its pillow, laid the child down again, and covered it with a little quilt. And she did not forget the roebuck, but went into the corner where it lay, and stroked its back. Then she went silently out of the door again. The next morning the nurse asked the guards whether anyone had come into the palace during the night, but they answered, "No, we have seen no one."

She came thus many nights and never spoke a word. The nurse always saw her, but she did not dare to tell anyone about it.

When some time had passed in this manner, the Queen began to speak in the night, and said,

> "How fares my child? How fares my deer?
> Oh, twice more only shall I come here."

The nurse did not answer, but when the Queen had gone again, went to the King and told him all. The King said, "Ah, heavens! What is this? Tomorrow night I will watch by the child myself."

In the evening he went into the nursery, and at midnight the Queen again appeared and said,

> "How fares my child? How fares my deer?
> Oh, once more only shall I come here."

And she nursed the child as usual before she went away. The King

129

dared not speak to her, but on the next night he watched again. Then she said,

> "How fares my child ? How fares my deer ?
> Oh, never again shall I come here."

Then the King could not restrain himself; he sprang towards her, and said, "You can be none other than my dear wife."

She answered, "Yes, I am your dear wife," and at the same moment she came to life again – fresh, rosy and full of health.

Then she told the King the evil deed which the wicked witch and her daughter had been guilty of towards her. The King ordered both to be led before the judge, and judgment was delivered against them. The daughter was taken into the forest where she was torn to pieces by wild beasts, but the witch was cast into the fire and miserably burnt. And as soon as she was burnt, the roebuck changed his shape, and received his human form again, so the sister and brother lived happily together all their lives.

The Turnip

There were once two brothers who both served as soldiers; one of them was rich, and the other poor. The poor one, to escape from his poverty, put off his soldier's coat, and turned farmer. He dug and hoed his bit of land, and sowed it with turnip-seed. The seed came up, and one turnip grew there which was enormous, and it went on growing bigger and bigger as if it would never stop, so that it might have been called the Queen of turnips, for its like had never been seen before, nor will it ever be seen again.

At length it was so huge that it filled a whole cart, and two oxen were required to draw it. The farmer had not the least idea what to do with the turnip or whether it would prove a fortune to him or a misfortune. At last he thought, "If I sell it, what shall I gain? If I eat it – why, small turnips would be just as good. It would be better to take it to the King, and make him a present of it."

So he placed it on a cart, harnessed two oxen, took it to the palace, and presented it to the King.

"What strange thing is this?" said the King. "Never have I seen such a monster as this! From what seed can this have sprung, or are you a luck-child and have met with it by chance?"

"Ah, no!" said the farmer. "No luck-child am I. I am a poor soldier, who because he could no longer support himself hung his soldier's

131

coat on a nail and took to farming. I have a brother who is rich and well known to you, Lord King, but I, because I have nothing, am forgotten by everyone."

Then the King pitied him and said, "I will end your poverty, and give you gifts to make you as rich as your brother."

So he bestowed on him much gold, and lands, and meadows, and herds, and made him immensely rich, so that the wealth of the other brother could not be compared with his. When the rich brother heard what the poor one had gained for himself with one single turnip, he envied him, and thought how he could have a similar piece of luck. He decided to set about it in a much wiser way, and took gold and horses and carried them to the King, feeling certain that the King would give him a much larger present in return. If his brother had got so much for one turnip, what would he not carry away with him in return for such beautiful things as these?

The King accepted his presents and said he had nothing to give him in return that was more rare and excellent than the great turnip. So the rich man was obliged to put his brother's turnip in a cart and have it taken to his home. Once there he did not know on whom to vent his rage and anger, until bad thoughts came to him, and he resolved to kill his brother. He hired murderers, who were to lie in ambush, and then he went to his brother and said, "Dear brother, I know of a hidden treasure. We'll dig it up together, and divide it between us."

His brother accompanied him without suspicion. While they were on their way, however, the murderers fell on him, bound him, and would have hanged him to a tree. But just as they were doing this, loud singing and the sound of a horse's hooves were heard in the distance. Terrified, they pushed their prisoner head first into a sack, hung it on a branch, and took to flight.

The farmer worked until he had made a hole in the sack through which he could put his head. The man who was coming by was a travelling student, a young fellow who rode through the wood joyously singing. When the man saw him he cried, "Good day! You have come in the nick of time."

The student looked round on every side, trying to see where the voice came from. At last he said, "Who calls me?"

Then an answer came from the top of the tree. "Raise your eyes; here I sit aloft in the Sack of Wisdom. In a short time I have learnt great things; compared with this all schools are a jest. Soon I shall have learnt everything, and shall descend wiser than all other men. I understand the stars, and the signs of the zodiac, and the tracks of the winds, the sand of the sea, the healing of illness, and the virtues of all herbs, birds, and stones. If you were once within it you would feel what wonders flow from the Sack of Wisdom."

The student, when he heard all this, was astonished, and said, "Blessed be the hour when I met you! May I enter the sack for a while?" The farmer in the sack replied as if unwillingly, "For a short time I will let you get into it, if you reward me; but you must wait an hour, for one thing remains which I must learn first."

When the student had waited a while he became impatient, and begged to be allowed to get in at once, his thirst for knowledge was so great. So the man in the sack pretended at last to yield, and said, "In order that I may get out you must let down the sack by the rope, and then you can get in."

So the student let the sack down, untied it, and set him free, and then cried, "Now draw me up at once," and was about to get into the sack.

"Stop!" said the other. "That won't do," and took him by the head and put him upside down into the sack, fastened it, and drew the disciple of wisdom up the tree by the rope. Then he swung him in the air and said, "How goes it with you, my dear fellow? You can feel wisdom coming upon you already and you are gaining valuable experience. Keep perfectly quiet until you become wiser."

Thereupon he mounted the student's horse and rode away, but in an hour's time sent someone to let the student out again.

Jorinda
and Joringel

There was once an old castle in the midst of a large and thick forest, and in it an old witch dwelt all alone. In the daytime she changed herself into a cat or a screech-owl, but in the evening she took her proper shape again as a human being. She could lure wild beasts and birds to her, and then she killed and boiled or roasted them. If anyone came within one hundred paces of the castle he was obliged to stand still, and could not stir from the place until she released him. But whenever an innocent maiden came within this circle, she changed her into a bird, and shut her up in a wickerwork cage, and carried the cage into a room in the castle. She had about seven thousand cages of rare birds in the castle.

Now, there was a maiden called Jorinda. She was fairer than all other girls. She and a handsome youth named Joringel had promised to marry each other. While they were betrothed, their greatest happiness was being together. One day in order to be alone they went for a walk in the forest. "Take care," said Joringel, "that we don't go too near the castle."

It was a beautiful evening; the sun slanted its beams between the trunks of the trees into the dark green of the forest, and the turtle-doves sang mournfully. Jorinda and Joringel looked around them, and were

quite at a loss, for they did not know the way home. Half the sun was still above the mountain and half had sunk below it.

Joringel looked through the bushes, and saw the old walls of the castle close at hand. He was horror-stricken and filled with deadly fear. Jorinda was singing,

> *"My little bird, with the necklace red,*
> *Sings sorrow, sorrow, sorrow,*
> *He sings that the dove must soon be dead,*
> *Sings sorrow, sorr--- jug, jug, jug."*

Joringel looked at Jorinda. She was changed into a nightingale, and sang "Jug, jug, jug." A screech-owl with glowing eyes flew three times round about her, and three times cried, "To-whoo, to-whoo, to-whoo!"

Joringel could not move: he stood there like a stone, and could neither weep nor speak, nor move hand or foot.

The sun had now set. The owl flew into the thicket, and directly afterwards there came out of it a crooked old woman, yellow and lean, with large red eyes and a hooked nose, the point of which reached to her chin. She caught the nightingale, and took it away in her hand, muttering,

> *"Till the prisoner's fast,*
> *And her doom is cast,*
> *There stay, O stay!*
> *When the charm is round her*
> *And the spell has bound her,*
> *Hie away, away!"*

Joringel could neither speak nor move from the spot; the nightingale was gone. At last the woman came back, and said in a hollow voice, "Greetings, Zachiel. If the moon shines on the cage, Zachiel, let him loose at once."

Then Joringel was freed. He fell on his knees before the woman and begged that she would give him back his Jorinda, but she said that he should never have her again, and went away. He called, he wept, he lamented, "Ah, what is to become of me?" but all in vain.

Joringel went away, and at last came to a strange village; there he tended sheep for a long time. He often walked round and round the castle, but not too near it. One night he dreamt that he found a star-blue flower, in the middle of which was a beautiful large pearl. He picked the flower and went with it to the castle, and everything he touched with the flower was freed from enchantment. He also dreamt that by means of it he recovered his Jorinda. In the morning, when he woke, he began to seek over hill and dale for such a flower. On the ninth day, early in the morning, he found the star-blue flower. In the middle of it there was a large dew-drop, as big as the finest pearl.

Day and night he journeyed with this flower to the castle. When he was within a hundred paces of it he was not held fast, but walked to the door. Joringel was full of joy; he touched the door with the flower, and it sprang open. He walked in through the courtyard, and listened for the sound of the birds. At last he heard it. He went on and found the room where the witch was feeding the birds in the seven thousand cages.

When she saw Joringel she was very angry, and snarled at him, but he took no notice of her, but went and searched among the cages. But among so many hundreds of nightingales, how was he to find his Jorinda again?

Then he saw the old woman quietly take away a cage with a bird in it, and go towards the door. He sprang swiftly towards her, touched the cage with the flower, and also the old woman. She no longer had the power to bewitch anyone; and Jorinda was standing there, clasping him round the neck, and as beautiful as ever! After that he changed all the other birds back into maidens again. Then he and Jorinda went home and lived together happily ever after.

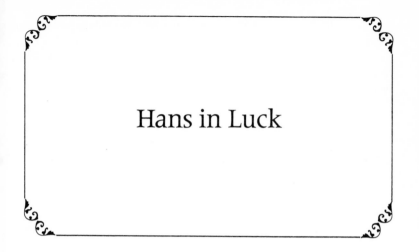

Hans in Luck

Hans had served his master for seven years, so he said to him, "Master, my time is up. I want to go back home to my mother; please give me my wages."

His master answered, "You have served me faithfully and honestly; as the service was, so shall the reward be"; and he gave Hans a piece of gold as big as his head. Hans pulled his handkerchief out of his pocket, wrapped the lump up in it, put it on his shoulder, and set off for home.

As he trudged on, dragging one foot after the other, he saw a horseman trotting merrily by on a lively horse.

"Ah!" said Hans. "What a fine thing it is to ride! There you sit as on a chair; you stumble over no stones, you save your shoes, and travel without any trouble."

The rider, who heard him, stopped and called out, "Hello, Hans, why do you go on foot, then?"

"I must," answered Hans, "for I have this lump to carry home. It's true that it's gold, but I can't hold my head straight because of it, and it hurts my shoulder."

"I'll tell you what," said the rider, "we'll exchange: I'll give you my horse, and you can give me your lump."

"With all my heart," said Hans, "But I can tell you, it's a heavy burden."

The rider got down, took the gold, and helped Hans up; then put the bridle in his hands and said, "If you want to go at a really good pace, you must click your tongue and call out 'Gee-up! Gee-up!'"

Hans was delighted to ride along on horseback with no effort. After a while he wanted to go faster, and he began to click with his tongue and call out "Gee-up! Gee-up!" The horse broke into a gallop, and before Hans knew where he was, he was thrown off and lying in a ditch. The horse would have run away if it had not been caught by a countryman, who was driving a cow along the highway.

Hans picked himself up, but he was angry, and said to the countryman, "Riding is no joke, especially on a mare like this, that stumbles and throws you off, so that you're likely to break your neck. Never again will I mount it. Now I like your cow, for you can walk quietly behind her, and besides that you get milk, butter, and cheese every day without fail. What wouldn't I give to have such a cow!"

"Well," said the countryman, "if it would give you so much pleasure, I don't mind giving the cow for the horse."

Hans agreed with the greatest delight; the countryman jumped on the horse, and rode quickly away. Hans drove his cow quietly before him, and thought over his lucky bargain. "If only I have a bit of bread – and surely I'll never be without that – I can eat butter and cheese with it as often as I like; if I'm thirsty, I can milk my cow and drink the milk. Goodness, what more can I want?"

When he came to an inn he made a halt, and in great content ate up what he had with him – his dinner and supper too – and with his last few coins bought half a glass of beer. Then he drove his cow along the road to his mother's village. As it drew nearer mid-day, the heat was more oppressive, and Hans found himself upon a moor. He felt very hot and his tongue stuck to the roof of his mouth with thirst.

"This is easily cured," thought Hans. "I will milk the cow and refresh myself with the milk."

He tied her to a withered tree, and as he had no pail he put his leather cap underneath, but try as he would, not a drop of milk came. And as he was clumsy, the impatient beast at last gave him such a blow on his head with its hind foot, that he fell to the ground, and for a long time could not think where he was. By good fortune a butcher just then came along the road with a wheelbarrow, in which lay a young pig.

"What's going on?" cried he, and helped Hans up. Hans told him what had happened. The butcher gave him his flask and said, "Take a drink and you'll feel better. That cow will certainly give no milk. It's an old beast – at best only fit for the plough, or for the butcher."

"Well, well," said Hans, "who would have thought it? I must say it's fine to have home-killed meat, but I don't care much for beef; it's not juicy enough for me. A young pig like that now is the thing to have; it tastes quite different; and then there are the sausages!"

"Listen, Hans," said the butcher. "Out of love for you I will exchange, and let you have the pig for the cow."

"Heaven repay you for your kindness!" said Hans as he gave up the cow. The pig was untied from the barrow, and its halter was put in his hand.

Hans went on, thinking how well things were going for him, with every problem put right. Presently he was joined by a lad carrying a fine white goose under his arm. They greeted each other, and Hans began to tell of his good luck, and of the bargains he had made. The boy told him that he was taking the goose to a christening-feast.

"Just lift her," he added, and held her up by the wings. "See how heavy she is – she has been fattened up for the last eight weeks. Whoever has a bit of her when she is roasted will have to wipe the fat from both sides of his mouth."

"Yes," said Hans, as he weighed her in one hand, "she is a good weight, but my pig is no bad one."

The lad looked suspiciously from side to side, and shook his head. "Look here," he said at length, "it may not be all right with your pig. In the village through which I passed, the Mayor himself had just had one stolen out of its sty. I fear – I fear that you have got hold of it there. They have sent out some people to look for it, and it would be a bad business if they caught you with the pig; at the very least, you would be shut up in the dark hole."

Poor Hans was terrified. "Goodness!" he said. "Please help me out of this fix. You know more about this place than I do; take my pig and leave me your goose."

"I shall be running a risk," answered the lad, "but I will not be the cause of your getting into trouble." So he took the halter in his hand, and drove the pig quickly along a by-path.

Hans, freed from care, went homewards with the goose under his arm. "When I think it over," said he to himself, "I have even gained by the exchange: first there is the delicious roast meat, then the quantity of fat which will drip from it, and give me dripping for my bread for a good three months; and lastly there are the beautiful white feathers. I can have my pillow stuffed with them, and then indeed I shall go to sleep without rocking. How glad my mother will be!"

As he was going through the last village, there stood a scissors-grinder with his barrow; as his wheel whirred he sang,

> "I sharpen scissors and quickly grind,
> My coat blows out in the wind behind."

Hans stood still and watched him. At last he spoke to him and said, "You must be doing well since you are so merry at your grinding."

"Yes," answered the scissors-grinder, "it's a trade with sound prospects. A real grinder is a man who when he puts his hand in his pocket always finds gold in it. But where did you buy that fine goose?"

"I did not buy it, but exchanged my pig for it."

"And the pig?"

"That I got for a cow."

"And the cow?"

"I took that instead of a horse."

"And the horse?"

"For that I gave a lump of gold as big as my head."

"And the gold?"

"Well, that was my wages for seven years' service."

"You have certainly known how to look after yourself each time," said the grinder. "If you can only manage to hear money jingle in your pockets whenever you stand up, you will have made your fortune."

"How shall I set about that?" asked Hans.

"You must be a grinder like me. Nothing particular is needed for it but a whetstone. The rest comes of itself. I have one here. It's certainly a little worn, but you needn't give me anything for it but your goose. Do you agree?"

"How can you ask?" answered Hans. "I shall be the luckiest fellow on earth. If I have money whenever I put my hand in my pocket, what more need I trouble about?" and he handed him the goose and received the whetstone in exchange.

"Now," said the grinder, as he took up an ordinary heavy stone that lay by him, "here is a strong stone for you into the bargain. You can hammer out your old nails on it to straighten them. Take it with you and keep it carefully."

Hans loaded himself with the stones, and went on with a contented heart; his eyes shone with joy. "I must have been born lucky," he cried, "everything I want happens to me just as if I were a Sunday-child."

As he had been on his legs since daybreak, Hans began to feel tired. He was very hungry, too, for in his joy at the bargain over the cow he had eaten up all his store of food. It was an effort to drag himself along, and he was forced to stop every minute to rest; the stones, too, weighed him down dreadfully. He could not help thinking how nice it would be if he did not have to carry them any further.

He crept like a snail to a well in a field, to rest and refresh himself with a cool draught of water, but in order not to injure the stones by

145

sitting on them, he laid them carefully by his side on the edge of the well. Just as he stooped to drink, he slipped, pushed against the stones, and both of them fell into the water.

When Hans saw them with his own eyes sinking to the bottom, he jumped for joy, and then knelt down, and with tears in his eyes thanked God for having shown him this further favour, and relieved him from those heavy stones – the only things that troubled him – without his having any need to reproach himself.

"There is no man under the sun as lucky as I," he cried. With a light heart and nothing left to hinder him, he bounded home to his mother.

The Goose-Girl

Once upon a time there was a Queen whose husband had been dead for many years, and she had a beautiful daughter. When the princess grew up she was betrothed to a prince who lived in a distant land. When the time came for her to be married, and she had to journey into that distant kingdom, the Queen packed up for her many costly vessels of silver and gold, and rich clothes and jewels; in short, everything for a royal dowry, for she loved her child with all her heart. She sent, too, her maid-in-waiting to ride with her, and hand her over to the bride-groom. Each had a horse for the journey, but the horse of the King's daughter was called Falada, and could speak.

When the hour of parting had come, the Queen went into her bedroom, took a small knife and cut her finger until it bled. Then she held a white handkerchief to it and let three drops of blood fall on it. She gave it to her daughter and said, "Dear child, keep this carefully; it will be of service to you on your journey."

They took a sorrowful leave of each other. The princess put the handkerchief in her bosom, mounted her horse, and rode away. After she had ridden for a while, she was very thirsty and said to the maid, "Dismount, and take my golden cup to the stream, for I should like some water."

147

"If you are thirsty," said the waiting-maid, "get off your horse and kneel and drink from the stream. I don't choose to be your servant."

So in her great thirst the princess dismounted, leaned over the water in the stream and drank, and was not allowed to drink out of the golden cup. "Alas!" she said, and the three drops of blood answered, "If your mother knew this, her heart would break."

But the King's daughter was humble, said nothing, and mounted her horse again. She rode on some miles, but the day was warm, the sun scorched her, and she was thirsty once more. When they came to a stream she again cried to her waiting-maid, "Dismount, and give me some water in my golden cup," for she had long ago forgotten the girl's rudeness.

But the waiting-maid said still more haughtily, "If you wish to drink, get the water yourself. I don't choose to be your servant."

The King's daughter was so thirsty that she dismounted, bent over the flowing stream, wept and said, "Alas!" and the drops of blood again replied, "If your mother knew this, her heart would break."

As she was leaning over the stream, the handkerchief with the three drops of blood fell out of her bosom, and floated away on the water without her noticing, so great was her distress. The waiting-maid, however, had seen it, and rejoiced to think that she now had power over the bride, for since the princess had lost the drops of blood, she had become weak and powerless. So when she wanted to mount her horse, Falada, again, the waiting-maid said, "Falada is more suitable for me. My nag is good enough for you," and the princess had to give up her horse.

Then the waiting-maid, with many hard words, bade the princess exchange her royal robes for her own shabby clothes; and finally made her swear by the clear sky above her, that she would not say one word of this to anyone at the royal court. If the princess had not taken this oath she would have been killed on the spot. But Falada saw all this, and observed it well.

The waiting-maid now mounted Falada, and the true bride the nag, and so they travelled on, until at length they entered the royal palace.

There were great rejoicings when they reached the palace. The prince sprang forward and lifted the waiting-maid from her horse, thinking she was the princess. She was conducted upstairs, but the real princess was left standing below.

The old King looked out of the window and saw her standing in the courtyard, delicate and beautiful, and instantly went to the royal apartment, and asked the bride about the girl she had with her who was standing down below in the courtyard. Who was she?

"I picked her up on my way for a companion. Give the girl something to do – don't let her stand idle."

The old King had no work for her, so he said, "I have a little boy who tends the geese; she may help him." The boy was called Conrad, and the true bride had to help him to tend the geese.

Soon afterwards the false bride said to the prince, "Dearest husband, I beg you to do me a favour."

"I will do so most willingly," he answered.

"Then send for the knacker, and cut off the head of the horse on which I rode here, for it vexed me on the way."

In reality she was afraid that the horse might tell how she had behaved to the King's daughter. The prince promised that it should be done, and the faithful Falada was killed. This came to the ears of the real princess, and she secretly promised to pay the knacker a piece of gold if he would do a small service for her. There was a great dark-looking gateway in the town, through which morning and evening she had to pass with the geese. Would he nail up Falada's head on it, so that she might see him as she went by? The knacker's man promised, cut off the head, and nailed it fast above the dark gateway.

Early in the morning, when she and Conrad drove their flock beneath this gateway, she called out,

> "Falada, Falada, hanging high . . . ."

Then the head answered,

> "Princess, Princess, passing by,
> Alas, alas! if thy mother knew it,
> Sadly, sadly, her heart would rue it."

Then they went still further out of the town, and drove their geese into the country. And when they came to a meadow, she sat down

149

and unbound her hair which was like pure gold. Conrad was delighted at its brightness, and wanted to pluck out a few hairs. Then she said,

> *"Blow, breezes, blow!*
> *Let Conrad's hat go!*
> *Blow, breezes, blow!*
> *Let him after it go.*
> *O'er hills, dales and rocks,*
> *Away be it whirled*
> *Till the bright shining locks*
> *Are all combed and curled."*

Then a wind sprang up so strong that it blew Conrad's hat far away over the fields, and he was forced to run after it. When he came back she had finished combing her hair and was putting it up again, so he could not get a single hair. Then Conrad was angry, and would not speak to her. They tended the geese until the evening, and then they went home.

Next day when they were driving the geese out through the dark gateway, the maiden said,

> *"Falada, Falada, hanging high . . . ."*

Falada answered,

> *"Princess, Princess, passing by,*
> *Alas, alas! if thy mother knew it,*
> *Sadly, sadly, her heart would rue it."*

And she sat down again in the field, and began to comb out her hair, and Conrad ran and tried to clutch it, so she said in haste,

> *"Blow, breezes, blow!*
> *Let Conrad's hat go!*
> *Blow, breezes, blow!*
> *Let him after it go.*
> *O'er hills, dales and rocks,*
> *Away be it whirled*
> *Till the bright shining locks*
> *Are all combed and curled."*

Then the wind blew, and blew his hat off his head and far away, and Conrad was forced to run after it. When he came back, her hair was all put up again, and he couldn't get a single hair. And so they tended their geese till evening came. But in the evening after they had got home, Conrad went to the old King, and said, "I won't tend the geese with that girl any longer! She vexes me the whole day long."

Then the old King told him to say how she vexed him, and Conrad said, "In the morning when we pass beneath the dark gateway with the flock, there is a horse's head on the wall and she says to it,

> 'Falada, Falada, hanging high . . . .'

and the head replies,

> 'Princess, Princess, passing by,
> Alas, alas! if thy mother knew it,
> Sadly, sadly, her heart would rue it.'"

And Conrad went on to relate what happened on the goose pasture, and how he had had to chase his hat.

The old King commanded him to drive his flock out again next day, and as soon as morning came, he himself hid behind the dark gateway, and heard how the maiden spoke to the head of Falada. Then the King followed them into the country, and from a thicket in the meadow soon saw with his own eyes the goose-girl and the goose-boy bringing their flock. After a while she sat down and unplaited her hair, which glittered in the sunlight. And soon she said,

> "Blow, breezes, blow!
> Let Conrad's hat go!
> Blow, breezes, blow!
> Let him after it go.
> O'er hills, dales and rocks,
> Away be it whirled
> Till the bright shining locks
> Are all combed and curled."

Then a gust of wind carried off Conrad's hat, so that he had to run after it, while the maiden quietly went on combing and plaiting her
152

hair. The King saw it all. Then, still unseen, he went away. When the goose-girl came home in the evening, he called her aside, and asked why she did all these things.

"I dare not tell my sorrows to any human being, for I have sworn not to do so by the clear sky above me; if I had not done so, I should have lost my life."

The King pressed her to tell him her story, but could get nothing from her. Then said he, "If you will tell me nothing, tell your sorrows to the iron stove there," and he went away.

Then she crept into the stove, and began to weep, and poured out her whole heart, and said, "Here am I deserted by the whole world, and yet I am a King's daughter, and a false waiting-maid has by force brought me to such a pass that I have been compelled to put off my royal robes. And she has taken my place with my bridegroom, and I have to perform menial service as a goose-girl. If my mother knew, her heart would break."

The old King stood outside by the pipe of the stove, and heard all that she said. He came back again, and told her to come out of the stove. And he had her dressed in royal garments, and it was marvellous how beautiful she was! The old King summoned his son, and told him that he had got the false bride who was only a waiting-maid, but that the true one was standing there, the so-called goose-girl. The prince was charmed by her beauty and youth, and a great banquet was made ready to which all the people and all good friends were invited. At the head of the table sat the bridegroom with the King's daughter at one side of him, and the waiting-maid on the other, but the waiting-maid was dazzled, and did not recognize the princess in her brilliant array.

When they had eaten and drunk and were merry, the old King asked the waiting-maid a riddle: what does a person deserve who has deceived her master? Then the false bride said, "She deserves to be stripped naked, and put in a barrel which is studded inside with pointed nails. Two white horses should drag it through the streets till she is dead."

"You have pronounced your own sentence," said the old King, "and it will be carried out." Afterwards the prince married his true bride, and they reigned over their kingdom in peace and happiness.

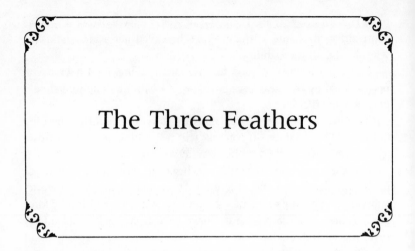

The Three Feathers

There was once a King who had three sons. Two were clever and wise, but the third did not speak much, and was simple, and was called the Simpleton. When the King grew old, he could not decide which of his sons should inherit the kingdom after him. So he said to them, "Go forth, and he who brings me the most beautiful carpet shall be King after my death." And so that there should be no dispute among them, he took them outside his castle, blew three feathers in the air, and said, "You shall go as they fly."

One feather flew to the east, and the other to the west, but the third flew straight up and did not fly far, but soon fell to the ground. One brother set out to the right, and the other to the left, and they mocked Simpleton, who was forced to stay where the third feather had fallen. He sat down feeling sad, when suddenly he saw a trap-door close by the feather. He raised it up, found some steps, and went down them. He came to another door, knocked at it, and heard somebody inside calling,

> "Little green maiden small,
> Hopping hither and thither,
> Hop quickly to the door,
> And see who's there."

The door opened, and he saw a great, fat toad sitting, with a crowd of little toads around her. The fat toad asked what he wanted.

"I am looking for the prettiest and finest carpet in the world," he answered.

Then she called a young one and said,

> *"Little green maiden small,*
> *Hopping hither and thither,*
> *Hop quickly and bring me*
> *The great box here."*

The young toad brought the box, and the fat toad opened it, and gave Simpleton a carpet out of it, so beautiful and so fine, that no one on earth could have woven one like it. Simpleton thanked her, and went up the steps and home.

His brothers had thought him too stupid to find anything at all.

"Why should we give ourselves a great deal of trouble to search?" said they, and got some coarse handkerchiefs from the first shepherds' wives whom they met, and carried them home to the King.

When the King saw Simpleton's beautiful carpet he was astonished, and said, "If justice be done, the kingdom belongs to the youngest."

But the two others gave their father no peace, and said that it was impossible that Simpleton, whom they thought so stupid, should be King, and entreated him to make a new agreement with them.

Then the father said, "He who brings me the most beautiful ring shall inherit the kingdom," and led the three brothers out, and blew into the air three feathers as before. Those of the two eldest again went east and west, and Simpleton's feather flew straight up, and fell down near the door in the earth.

Then he went down again to the fat toad, and told her that he wanted the most beautiful ring. She at once ordered her great box to be brought, and gave him a ring out of it, which sparkled with jewels, and was so beautiful that no goldsmith on earth would have been able to make it.

The two eldest mocked at Simpleton for going to seek a golden ring. They took no trouble, but knocked the nails out of an old carriage-ring, and took it to the King. But when Simpleton produced his golden

155

ring, his father again said, "The kingdom belongs to him." The two eldest gave the King no peace until he made a third agreement, and declared that the one who brought the most beautiful woman home should have the kingdom. He again blew the three feathers into the air, and they flew as before.

Then Simpleton without more ado went down to the fat toad, and said, "I am to take home the most beautiful woman!"

"Oh," answered the toad, "the most beautiful woman! She is not at hand at the moment, but still you shall have her."

She gave him a yellow turnip which had been hollowed out, to which six mice were harnessed.

Then Simpleton said sadly, "Whatever am I to do with that?"

"Just put one of my little toads into it," the toad answered.

Simpleton seized one at random out of the circle, and put her into the yellow turnip, but hardly was she seated inside it than she turned into a wonderfully beautiful maiden, and the turnip into a coach, and the six mice into horses. So he kissed her, and drove off quickly with her to the King.

Later his brothers came; they had taken no trouble at all to seek beautiful girls, but each had brought the first peasant woman he chanced to meet.

When the King saw them he said, "After my death the kingdom belongs to my youngest son." But the two eldest deafened the King's ears afresh with their protests. "We cannot consent to Simpleton's being King," they stormed, and demanded that the one whose wife could leap through a ring which hung in the centre of the hall should be the heir. They thought, "The peasant women can do that easily; they are strong, but the delicate maiden will jump herself to death." The old King agreed to their suggestion. Then the two peasant women jumped through the ring, but were so stout that they fell and their coarse arms and legs broke in two. But the pretty maiden whom Simpleton had brought with him sprang and sprang through as lightly as a deer, and this settled the matter. So Simpleton received the crown, and ruled wisely for many, many years.

The Poor Man
and the
Rich Man

In olden times, when the Lord himself still used to walk about on this earth, it once happened that he was tired and overtaken by darkness before he could reach an inn. Now there stood on the road before him two houses facing each other; the one large and beautiful, the other small and poor. The large one belonged to a rich man, and the small one to a poor man.

Then the Lord thought, "I shall be no burden to the rich man. I will stay the night with him." When the rich man heard someone knocking at his door, he opened the window and asked the stranger what he wanted. The Lord answered, "I only ask for a night's lodging."

The rich man looked the traveller over from head to foot, and as the Lord was wearing common clothes, and did not look like one who had much money in his pocket, he shook his head, and said, "No, I cannot take you in. My rooms are full of herbs and seeds; and if I were to lodge everyone who knocked at my door, I might very soon go begging myself. Go somewhere else for a lodging." With this he shut down the window and left the Lord standing there.

So the Lord turned his back on the rich man, and went across to the small house and knocked. He had hardly done so when the poor man opened the little door and bade the traveller come in.

"Pass the night with me; it is already dark," said he, "You cannot go any further tonight."

This pleased the Lord, and he went in. The poor man's wife shook hands with him, and welcomed him, and said he was to make himself at home and share what they had got; they had not much to offer him, but what they had they would give him with all their hearts. Then she put the potatoes on the fire, and while they were boiling, she milked the goat, that they might have a little milk with them.

When the cloth was laid, the Lord sat down with the man and his wife, and he enjoyed their coarse food, for there were happy faces at the table. When they had had supper and it was bedtime, the woman called her husband apart and said, "Hark you, dear husband, let us make up a bed of straw for ourselves tonight, and then the poor traveller can sleep in our bed and have a good rest, for he has been walking the whole day through, and must be weary."

"With all my heart," he answered. "I will go and offer it to him." And he went to the stranger and invited him to sleep in their bed and rest his limbs properly. But the Lord was unwilling to take their bed from the two old folks; however, they would not be satisfied, until at length he lay down in their bed, while they themselves lay on some straw on the ground.

Next morning they got up before daybreak, and made as good a breakfast as they could for the guest. When the sun shone in through the little window, the Lord again ate with them, and then prepared to set out on his journey. But as he was standing at the door he turned round and said, "As you are so kind and good, you may wish three things for yourselves and I will grant them."

Then the man said, "What else would I wish for but eternal happiness, and that we two, as long as we live, may be healthy and have every day our daily bread. For the third wish, I do not know what to have."

And the Lord said to him, "Will you wish for a new house instead of this old one?"

"Oh, yes," said the man. "If I can have that too, I should like it very much."

And the Lord fulfilled his wish, and changed their old house into a new one, again gave them his blessing, and went on his way.

The sun was high when the rich man got up and leaned out of his window and saw, on the opposite side of the street, a new house with red tiles and bright windows where the old hut used to be. He was very much astonished, and calling his wife said, "Tell me, what can have happened? Last night there was a miserable little hut standing there, and today there is a beautiful new house. Run over and see how that has come to pass."

So his wife went and asked the poor man, and he said to her, "Yesterday evening a traveller came here and asked for a night's lodging, and this morning when he took leave of us he granted us three wishes – eternal happiness, health and our daily bread as well, and, besides this, a beautiful new house instead of our old hut."

When the rich man's wife heard this, she ran back in haste and told her husband. The man said, "I could tear myself to pieces! If I had but known that! The traveller came to our house too, and wanted to sleep here, and I sent him away."

"Quick!" said his wife. "Get on your horse. You can still catch the man up, and then you must ask to have three wishes granted you."

The rich man followed the good counsel and galloped away on his horse, and soon came up with the Lord. He spoke to him softly and pleasantly, and begged him not to take it amiss that he had not let him in directly. He had been looking for the front door key, and meanwhile the stranger had gone away. If he returned the same way he must come and stay with him.

"Yes," said the Lord, "if I ever come back again, I will do so."

Then the rich man asked if he might not wish for three things too, as his neighbour had done.

The Lord said he might, but it would not be to his advantage, and that he had better not wish for anything; but the rich man thought that he could easily ask for something which would add to his happiness, if he only knew that it would be granted. So the Lord said to him, "Ride home, then, and your three wishes will be granted."

The rich man rode home, and began to think what he should wish for. As he was thinking he let the bridle fall, and the horse began to caper about, so that he could not collect his thoughts at all. He patted its neck, and said, "Gently, Lisa," but the horse only began new tricks. At last he was angry, and cried impatiently, "I wish your neck was broken!"

Directly he had said the words, the horse fell to the ground, and there it lay dead and never moved again. And thus was his first wish granted. As he was miserly by nature, he did not like to leave the harness lying there; so he cut it off, and put it on his back; and now he had to go on foot. "I still have two wishes left," said he, and comforted himself with that thought.

As he was walking slowly through the sand, with the sun burning hot at noonday, he grew angry. The saddle hurt his back, and he had still no idea what to wish for. "If I were to wish for all the riches and treasures in the world," said he to himself, "I know I should regret all the things I had *not* wished for. So I must choose so that there is nothing at all left for me to wish for afterwards."

Many a time he thought he had found the right wish, but then it came into his mind what an easy life his wife had, for she stayed at home in a cool room and enjoyed herself. This really did vex him, and without thinking, he said, "I just wish she was sitting here on this saddle, and could not get off it, instead of my having to drag it along on my back." As the last word was spoken, the saddle disappeared from his back, and he saw that his second wish had been granted. Then he really did feel panic stricken. He began to run. But when he got home and opened the parlour door, he saw his wife sitting in the middle of the room on the saddle, crying and complaining – she was stuck fast on it!

"If only you will endure this," he said, "and stay fixed to the saddle, I will wish for all the riches on earth for you."

She, however, called him a fool, and said, "What good will all the riches on earth do me, if I am to sit on this saddle? You have wished me on it, and you must wish me off."

So whether he would or not, he was forced to let his third wish be that she should be quit of the saddle, and able to get off it, and immediately the wish was granted. So he got nothing by it but vexation, trouble, abuse, and the loss of his horse; but the poor people lived happily for the rest of their lives.

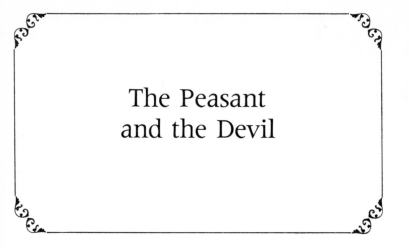

The Peasant
and the Devil

Once upon a time there was a far-sighted, crafty peasant whose tricks were much talked about, and especially the story of how he once made a fool of the Devil.

The peasant had one day been working in his field, and as twilight set in was making ready for the journey home, when he saw a heap of burning coals in the middle of his field. When, full of astonishment, he went up to it, a little black devil was sitting on the live coals.

"You do indeed sit upon a treasure!" said the peasant.

"Yes, in truth," replied the Devil, "on a treasure which contains more gold and silver than you have ever seen in your life!"

"The treasure lies in my field and belongs to me," said the peasant.

"It is yours," answered the Devil, "if you will for two years give me half of everything your field produces. Money I have enough of, but I have a desire for the fruits of the earth."

The peasant agreed to the bargain. "In order, however, that no dispute may arise about the division," said he, "everything that is above ground shall belong to you, and what is under the earth to me."

The Devil was quite satisfied with that, but the cunning peasant had sown turnips.

Now when the time for harvest came, the Devil appeared and wanted to take away his crop; but he found nothing above ground but the yellow

163

withered leaves, while the peasant, full of delight, was digging up his turnips.

"You win this time," said the Devil, "but next time I shall win. What grows above ground shall be yours, and what is under it, mine."

"I'm willing," replied the peasant; but when the time came to sow, he did not sow turnips, but wheat. The grain became ripe, and the peasant went into the field and cut the full stalks down to the ground. When the Devil came, he found nothing but the stubble, and went away in a fury down into a cleft in the rocks.

"That's the way to cheat the Devil," said the peasant, and went and fetched away the treasure.

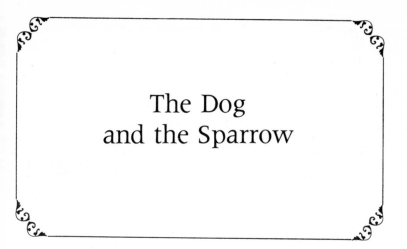

The Dog
and the Sparrow

A sheep dog had a master who took no care of him, but often let him go hungry. At last he could bear it no longer; so he took to his heels, and off he ran in a very sad and sorrowful mood. On the road he met a sparrow who said to him, "Why are you so sad, my friend?"

"Because," said the dog, "I am very, very hungry, and have nothing to eat."

"If that's all," answered the sparrow, "come with me into the next town, and I will soon find you plenty of food."

So on they went together into the town; and as they passed by a butcher's shop, the sparrow said to the dog, "Stand there a moment till I peck you down a piece of meat."

The sparrow perched on the counter and having first looked carefully about to see if anyone was watching, she pecked and scratched at a steak that lay on the edge of the counter, till at last it fell. The dog soon gobbled it all up.

"Come with me to the next shop," said the sparrow, "and I will peck you down another steak."

When the dog had eaten this too, the sparrow said, "Well, my friend, have you had enough now?"

"I've had plenty of meat," he answered, "but I should like a piece of bread to eat after it."

"Come with me," said the sparrow, "and you shall soon have that too."

So she took him to a baker's shop, and pecked at two rolls that lay in the window till they fell down; and as the dog still wanted more, she took him to another shop and pecked down more for him. When that was eaten, the sparrow asked him whether he had had enough now.

"Yes," said he; "and now let's take a walk a little way out of the town."

So they went out upon the high road; but as the weather was warm, they had not gone far before the dog said, "I'm very tired; I'd like to take a nap."

"Very well," answered the sparrow, "do so, and in the meantime I'll perch upon that bush."

So the dog stretched himself out on the road, and fell fast asleep. While he slept, there came by a carter with a cart drawn by three horses, and loaded with two casks of wine. The sparrow, seeing that the carter did not turn aside, but continued in the track in which the dog lay, and would drive over him, called out, "Stop! Stop! Mr Carter, or it will be the worse for you."

But the carter, grumbling to himself, "How can you make it the worse for me, indeed!" cracked his whip, and drove his cart over the poor dog, so that the wheels crushed him to death.

"There," cried the sparrow, "you cruel villain, you have killed my friend the dog. This cruelty of yours will cost you all that you own."

"Do your worst, and welcome," said the carter. "What harm can you do me?" and passed on.

But the sparrow crept under the tarpaulin of the cart, and pecked at the bung of one of the casks till she loosened it; and then all the wine ran out, without the carter seeing it. At last he looked round, and saw that the cart was dripping, and the cask quite empty.

"What an unlucky wretch I am!" cried he.

"Not wretch enough yet!" said the sparrow, as she alighted upon the head of one of the horses, and pecked at him till he reared up and kicked. When the carter saw this, he drew out his hatchet and aimed a blow at the sparrow, meaning to kill her; but she flew away, and

166

the blow fell upon the poor horse's head with such force that he fell down dead.

"Unlucky wretch that I am!" cried the carter.

"Not wretch enough yet!" said the sparrow. And as the carter went on with the other two horses, she again crept under the tarpaulin of the cart, and pecked out the bung of the second cask, so that all the wine ran out.

When the carter saw this, he again cried out, "Miserable wretch that I am!" But the sparrow answered, "Not wretch enough yet!" and perched on the head of the second horse, and pecked at him too. The carter ran up and struck at her again with his hatchet; but away she flew, and the blow fell upon the second horse, and killed him on the spot.

167

"Unlucky wretch that I am!" said the carter.

"Not wretch enough yet!" said the sparrow, and perching upon the third horse, she began to peck him too. The carrier was mad with fury; and without looking about him, or caring what he was about, struck again at the sparrow, but killed his third horse as he had done the other two.

"Alas! miserable wretch that I am!" cried he

"Not wretch enough yet!" answered the sparrow as she flew away. "Now I am going to bring poverty to you in your own home."

The carter was forced at last to leave his cart behind him, and to go home bursting with rage and vexation.

"Alas!" he said to his wife. "What ill luck I have had today. My wine is all spilt, and my horses all three dead."

"Alas! husband," replied she, "and a wicked bird has come into the house, and has brought with her all the birds in the world, I'm sure, and they have fallen upon our corn in the loft, and are eating it up at such a rate!"

Away ran the husband upstairs, and saw thousands of birds sitting upon the floor eating up his corn, with the sparrow in the midst of them.

"Unlucky wretch that I am!" cried the carter; for he saw that the corn was almost gone.

"Not wretch enough yet!" said the sparrow. "Your cruelty will cost you your life!" and away she flew.

The carter, seeing that he had lost all that he had, went down into his kitchen; and was still not sorry for what he had done, but sat himself angrily and sulkily in the chimney corner. But the sparrow sat on the outside of the window, and cried, "Carter! Your cruelty will cost you your life!"

With that he jumped up in a rage, seized his hatchet, and threw it at the sparrow; but it missed her, and only broke the window. The sparrow now hopped in, perched upon the window-seat, and cried, "Carter! It will cost you your life!"

Then the carter became blind with rage, and struck the window-seat with such force that he split it in two. As the sparrow flew from place to place, the carter and his wife were so furious that they broke all their

furniture, glasses, chairs, benches, the table, and at last the walls, without touching the bird at all. In the end, however, they caught her, and the wife said, "Shall I kill her at once?"

"No," cried he, "that is letting her off too easily: she shall die a much more cruel death; I will eat her," and he swallowed her at a gulp.

But the sparrow began to flutter about inside him, and she flew up into his mouth and cried, "Carter! It will cost you your life yet!"

With that he could wait no longer; so he gave his wife the hatchet, and cried, "Wife, strike at the bird and kill her." And the wife struck; but she missed her aim, and hit her husband on the head so that he fell down dead, and the sparrow flew quietly home to her nest.

The Valiant
Little Tailor

One summer's morning a little tailor was sitting on his table by the window. He was in good spirits, and sewed with all his might. A peasant woman came down the street crying, "Good jams, cheap! Good jams, cheap!" The tailor put his pale face out of the window, and called, "Come up, good woman; you will soon sell your wares here."

The woman came up the three steps to the tailor with her heavy basket, and he made her unpack all the pots for him. He inspected each of them, put his nose to them, and at length said, "The jam seems all right, so weigh me out four ounces, good woman, and if it is over the quarter of a pound, it's all the same to me."

The woman, who had hoped to sell a lot of jam, gave him what he asked for, but went away angry and grumbling.

"Now, God bless the jam to my use," cried the little tailor, "and give me health and strength." He brought some bread out of the cupboard, cut a slice and spread the jam on it. "There," he said, "I'll just finish the jacket before I take a bite."

He laid the bread near him, sewed on, and in his eagerness made bigger and bigger stitches. In the meantime the smell of the jam attracted the flies on the wall. They flew down and settled on the jam in hosts.

"Hello! Who invited you?" said the little tailor, and drove the unbidden guests away. The flies, however, came back in ever increasing hordes.

The little tailor at last lost all patience. He got a bit of cloth from the hole under his work-table, and saying, "I'll give you what for," struck at them mercilessly. When he counted, there lay before him no fewer than seven dead, with legs stretched out.

"So that's the kind of fellow you are," said he, and could not help admiring his own bravery. "The whole town shall know of this!" And the little tailor hastened to cut himself a girdle, stitched it, and embroidered on it in large letters, "Seven at one stroke!"

"What, only the town?" he continued. "The whole world shall hear of it!" The tailor put on the girdle, and resolved to go forth into the world, because he thought his workshop was too small for his valour. Before he went away, he looked about to see if there was anything which he could take with him. He found nothing but an old cheese, and that he put in his pocket.

In front of the door he saw a bird caught in a thicket. He put it into his pocket with the cheese. He took to the road boldly, and as he was light and nimble, he felt no fatigue. The road led him up a mountain, and when he had reached the highest point of it, there sat a powerful giant. The little tailor went bravely up and said, "Good day, comrade, you sit there surveying the world on every side! I am just off to try my luck. Do you feel inclined to go with me?"

The giant looked contemptuously at the tailor, and said, "You ragamuffin! You miserable creature!"

"Oh, indeed?" answered the little tailor. He unbuttoned his coat, and showed the giant the girdle. "Here you may read what kind of man I am!"

The giant read, "Seven at one stroke" and thought it was men whom the tailor had killed, and began to feel respect for the tiny fellow. Nevertheless, he thought he would test him, and took a stone in his hand, and squeezed it so that water dropped out of it. "Do that," said the giant, "if you have strength!"

"Is that all?" said the tailor. "That's child's play for me!" and he put his hand in his pocket, brought out the soft cheese, and pressed it until the liquid ran out of it.

"How's that?" said he.

The giant did not know what to say, and could not have believed it of the little man. The giant picked up a stone and threw it so high that the eye could scarcely follow it. "Now, little manikin, beat that if you can."

"Well thrown," said the tailor, "but after all the stone came down to earth again. I will throw you one which will never come back at all," and he put his hand into his pocket, took out the bird, and threw it into the air. The bird, delighted with its liberty, rose, flew away and did not come back.

"How's that, comrade?" asked the tailor.

"You can certainly throw," said the giant, "but now we'll see if you can carry anything of weight."

He took the little tailor to a mighty oak tree which lay felled on the ground, and said, "If you are strong enough, help me to carry the tree out of the forest."

"Willingly," answered the little man. "You take the trunk on your shoulders, and I will take the branches and twigs; after all, they are the heaviest."

The giant took the trunk on his shoulder, but the tailor seated himself on a branch, and the giant who could not look round had to carry away the whole tree, and the little tailor into the bargain. The tailor, perched at the end of the tree, whistled merrily as if carrying the tree were child's play. The giant, after he had dragged the heavy burden some way, could go no further, and cried, "Look out, I'll have to let the tree fall!"

The tailor sprang nimbly down, seized the tree with both arms as if he had been carrying it all the time, and said, "Fancy a great fellow like you not being able to carry a tree!"

They went on together, and as they passed a cherry tree, the giant laid hold of the top of the tree where the ripest fruit was hanging, bent it down, put it into the tailor's hand, and told him to eat. But the little tailor was much too weak to hold the tree, and when the giant let it go, it sprang back again, and the tailor shot into the air with it. When he reached the ground again without injury, the giant said, "What's this? Haven't you strength enough to hold a weak twig?"

"It's not lack of strength," answered the little tailor. "That's nothing to a man who has struck down seven at one blow. I leapt over the tree because the huntsmen are shooting down there in the thicket. See if you can jump like that."

The giant leapt, but could not clear the tree, and remained hanging in the branches. Once more the tailor had the better of him.

The giant said, "If you are such a valiant fellow, come with me into our cavern, and spend the night with us."

The little tailor was willing, and followed him. When they went into the cave, other giants were sitting by the fire, and each of them had a roasted sheep in his hand and was eating it. The giant showed him a bed, and said he was to lie down on it and sleep. The bed was, however, too big for the little tailor, so he did not lie on it but crept into a corner. At midnight, when the giant thought that the little tailor was sound asleep, he got up, took a great iron bar, sliced through the bed with one blow, and thought he had finished off the little man. At dawn the giants went into the forest, and had quite forgotten the little tailor, when all at once he walked up to them boldly. The giants were terrified: they were afraid that he would strike them all dead, and ran away in a great hurry.

The little tailor went on his way, always following his own pointed nose. After he had walked for a long time, he came to the courtyard of a royal palace, and as he felt weary, he lay down on the grass and fell asleep. While he slept, the people came and inspected him, and read on his girdle, "Seven at one stroke."

"Ah!" they said. "He must be a mighty warrior."

They went and told the King about him, and gave it as their opinion that if war should break out, he would be a useful man who ought on no account to be allowed to depart. So the King sent one of his courtiers to the little tailor to offer him military service. The ambassador remained standing by the sleeper, waited until he stretched his limbs and opened his eyes, and then made him this offer.

"For this very reason have I come here," the tailor said. "I am ready to enter the King's service." He was therefore received with honour, and a separate dwelling was assigned him.

The soldiers, however, were ill-disposed to the little tailor, and wished him a thousand miles away. "What is to be the end of this?" they said among themselves. "If we quarrel with him, and he strikes out, seven of us will fall at every blow. Not one of us can stand against him."

They came therefore to a decision, went to the King, and begged for their dismissal. "We are not prepared," said they, "to stay with a man who kills seven at one stroke." The King was sorry to lose all his faithful servants for the sake of one, wished that he had never set eyes on the tailor, and would willingly have been rid of him. But he did not dare dismiss him, lest he should strike him and all his people dead, and place himself on the royal throne.

He thought about it for a long time, and at last devised a plan. He sent for the little tailor and told him that as he was such a great warrior, he had a request to make. In the forest in his country lived two giants, who caused great mischief with their robbing, murdering, ravaging, and burning, and no one could approach them without risking death. If the tailor killed these two giants, he would give him his only daughter to wife, and half of his kingdom as a dowry. One hundred horsemen should go with him to assist him.

"That would indeed be a fine thing for a man like me!" thought the little tailor. "A beautiful princess and half a kingdom don't come my way every day! Oh yes," he told the King, "I'll soon subdue the giants, and don't require the help of the hundred horsemen. He who slays seven with one blow has no need to be afraid of two!"

The little tailor set out, and the hundred horsemen followed him. When he came to the outskirts of the forest, he said to his followers, "Just wait here. I alone will soon finish off the giants." Then he bounded into the forest and looked about. After a while he saw both giants. They lay sleeping under a tree, and snored so that the branches waved up and down. The little tailor, who was no fool, gathered two pocketsful of stones and climbed up the tree. When he was halfway up, he slid on to a branch just above the sleepers, and dropped one stone after another on the breast of one of them. For a long time the giant felt nothing, but at last he awoke, pushed his comrade and said, "What are you hitting me for?"

"You must be dreaming," said the other, "I'm not hitting you."

175

They lay down to sleep again, and then the tailor threw a stone down on the second.

"What is the meaning of this?" cried he. "Why are you pelting me?"

"I am not pelting you," answered the first, growling. They argued about it for some time, but as they were weary they let the matter rest, and their eyes closed once more. The little tailor began his game again, picked out the biggest stone, and threw it with all his might on the breast of the first giant.

"That's too much!" cried he, and sprang up like a madman. He pushed his companion against the tree until it shook. The other paid him back in the same coin, and they got into such a rage that they tore up trees and belaboured each other so fiercely that at last they both fell down dead on the ground. Then the little tailor leapt down.

"It's a lucky thing," said he, "that they did not tear up the tree on which I was sitting, or I should have had to spring on to another like a squirrel; but we tailors are nimble." He drew out his sword and gave each of them a couple of stabs in the heart, and then went out to the horsemen and said, "The work is done; I have given both of them their finishing stroke, but it was hard work! They tore up trees in their sore need to defend themselves, but all that's to no purpose when a man like myself comes, who can kill seven at one blow."

"But are you not wounded?" asked the horsemen.

"You need not worry about that," answered the tailor. "They have not hurt one hair of me."

The horsemen would not believe him, and rode into the forest to see. There they found the giants in pools of blood, and, round about them, the torn-up trees.

The little tailor demanded of the King the promised reward; but he repented of his promise, and again thought how he could get rid of the hero.

"Before I give you my daughter and half my kingdom," said he, "you must perform one more heroic deed. In the forest roams a unicorn which does great harm; you must catch it."

"I fear one unicorn still less than two giants," said the tailor. "Seven at one blow is more my style."

He took a rope and an axe with him, went into the forest, and again

176

told those who were sent with him to wait outside. Before long the unicorn appeared, and rushed at the tailor as if it meant to run him through with its horn.

"Softly, softly; it can't be done as quickly as that," said he. He waited until the animal was quite close, and then sprang nimbly behind a tree. The unicorn ran against the tree with all its strength, and drove its horn so fast into the trunk that it could not draw it out again, and so was caught.

"Now I have him safe!" said the tailor. He came out from behind the tree, put the rope round its neck, and then with his axe hewed the horn out of the tree. Then he led the beast to the King.

The King still would not give him the promised reward, and made a third demand. Before the wedding the tailor was to catch a wild boar that was making great havoc in the forest. The huntsmen were to help him.

"Willingly," said the tailor. "That will be child's play!"

He did not take the huntsmen with him into the forest, but went alone. When the boar saw the tailor, it ran at him with foaming mouth, gnashing its tusks, and was about to throw him to the ground, but the nimble hero sprang into a chapel which was near, and in one bound leapt out through the window again. The boar ran in after him, but the tailor ran round outside and shut the door behind it. And so the raging beast, which was much too heavy and clumsy to leap out of the window, was caught. The little tailor called the huntsmen to see the prisoner with their own eyes.

The King was now, whether he liked it or not, obliged to keep his promise, and gave the tailor his daughter and half of his kingdom. Had he known that it was no warlike hero, but a little tailor who was standing before him, he would have been still more upset. The wedding was held with great magnificence and small joy, and out of a tailor a king was made.

After some time the Queen heard her husband say in his sleep, "Boy, make me the doublet, and patch the pantaloons, or I will rap the yard-measure about your ears." Then she realized his humble origin, and next morning complained of her wrongs to her father, and begged him to help her to get rid of her husband, who was nothing but a

177

tailor. The King comforted her and said, "Leave your bedroom door open tonight, and my servants shall stand outside. When he has fallen asleep, they will go in, bind him, and take him on board a ship which will carry him far away." The lady was satisfied with this; but the King's armour-bearer, who had heard all, was friendly with the young King, and informed him of the whole plot.

"I'll soon put a stop to their plans," said the little tailor. At night he went to bed with his wife at the usual time, and when she thought that he had fallen asleep, she got up, opened the door, and then lay down again. The little tailor, who was only pretending to be asleep, began to cry out in a clear voice, "Boy, make me the doublet and patch me the pantaloons, or I will rap the yard-measure about your ears. I smote seven at one blow. I killed two giants, I brought away one unicorn, and caught a wild boar. Why should I fear those who are standing outside the room?"

When they heard the tailor speaking like this, the servants were terrified, and ran as if wild animals were after them, and none of them dared to plot any more against him. So the little tailor remained a king to the end of his life.

The Tom-Tit
and the Bear

Once in summer time the bear and the wolf were walking in the forest, and the bear heard a bird singing so beautifully that he said, "Brother Wolf, what bird is it that sings so well?"

"That is the King of birds," said the wolf, "before whom we must bow down."

But really it was the Tom-tit.

"If that's the case," said the bear, "I should very much like to see his royal palace. Can you take me there?"

"That's not as easy as you seem to think," said the wolf. "You must wait until the Queen comes."

Soon afterwards the Queen arrived with some food in her beak, and the lord King came too, and they began to feed their young ones. The bear would have liked to go in at once, but the wolf held him back by the sleeve, and said, "No, you must wait until the King and Queen fly away again."

So they marked the hole in which was the nest, and trotted away. The bear, however, could not rest until he had seen the royal palace, and before long he came back. The King and Queen had just flown out, so he peeped in and saw five or six young ones in the nest.

"Is that the royal palace?" cried the bear. "It is a wretched hole. You are not King's children, you are but base-born brats!"

When the young tom-tits heard that, they were furious, and cheeped angrily, "No, that we are not! Our parents are honest people! Bear, you will pay for this!"

The bear was frightened and ran back to his den. But the young tom-tits continued to cry and scream, and when their parents again brought food they said, "We won't touch even a fly's leg, no, not if we die of hunger, until you tell us whether we are your lawful children or not. The bear has been here and insulted us!"

Then the King said, "Only be quiet and he shall be punished." He at once flew with the Queen to the bear's den, and called in, "Old Growler, why have you insulted my children? You will pay for this."

So war against the bear was declared, and all four-footed animals were summoned to take part in it: oxen, asses, cows, deer, and every other animal on earth. And the tom-tit summoned everything which flew in the air, not only birds, large and small, but midges and hornets, bees, and flies.

When the time came for the war to begin, the tom-tit sent out spies to discover who was the enemy's commander-in-chief. The gnat, who was most crafty, flew into the forest where the enemy was assembled, and hid himself beneath a leaf of the tree where orders were to be given. There stood the bear, and he called the fox before him, and said, "Fox, you are the most cunning of all animals. You shall be general and lead us."

"Good," said the fox, "but what signal shall we agree upon?"

No one could think of one, so the fox said, "I have a fine bushy tail, which almost looks like a plume of red feathers. When I lift my tail up high, all is going well, and you must charge; but if I let it hang down, run away as fast as you can."

When the gnat heard this, she flew back again and told the tom-tit all she had heard. At daybreak, when the battle was to begin, all the four-footed animals came running up with such a noise that the earth trembled. The tom-tit too came flying through the air with his army with a humming, and whirring, and swarming that was terrifying to hear. Each side advanced against the other. But the tom-tit sent down the hornet, with orders to get beneath the fox's tail, and sting it with all his might. When the fox felt the first sting, up shot one leg in the

181

air with pain. But he bore it, and still kept his tail high. At the second sting, he was forced to lower it for a moment. At the third, he could hold out no longer. He yelped, and down went his tail between his legs. When the animals saw this they thought the battle was lost. They rushed helter skelter back to their dens. The birds had won!

Then the King and Queen flew home to their children and cried, "Children, rejoice! Eat and drink to your heart's content! We have won the battle!"

But the young tom-tits said, "We won't eat until the bear comes to the nest and begs for pardon and says that we are your lawful children."

Then the tom-tit flew to the bear's hole and cried, "Growler, you must come and apologise to my children, or else every rib of your body will be broken."

So the bear crept to the nest in great fear, and begged their pardon. At last the young tom-tits were satisfied, and ate and drank, and made merry till late into the night.

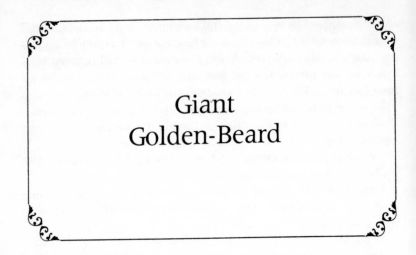

Giant
Golden-Beard

In a country village, over the hills and far away, lived a poor man, who had an only son. Now this child was born under a lucky star, and was therefore what the people of that country call a luckchild; and those who told his fortune said that in his fourteenth year he would marry no less a lady than the king's own daughter.

It so happened that the king, soon after the child's birth, passed through the village in disguise, and stopping at the blacksmith's shop, asked what news was stirring. "Good news!" said the people. "Master Brock, down that lane, has just had a son and they say he's a luckchild; and we're told that, when he's fourteen years old, he will marry our noble king's daughter."

This did not please the king; so he went to the child's parents, and asked them whether they would sell him their son? "No," said they. But the stranger begged very hard, and said he would give a great deal of money. So as they had all but nothing to eat, they at last agreed, saying to themselves, "He is a luckchild so no doubt everything is for the best – he can come to no harm."

The king took the baby, put it in a box, and rode away; but when he came to a deep stream he threw it into the current, and said to himself, "That young gentleman will never be my daughter's husband."

The box, however, floated down the stream. Some kind fairy watched over it, so that no water reached the child, and at last, about two miles from the king's city, it stopped at the dam of a mill. The miller soon saw it, took a long pole and drew it towards the shore. Finding it heavy, he thought there was gold inside; but when he opened it he found a pretty little boy that smiled upon him merrily. Now the miller and his wife had no children, and they therefore rejoiced to see their prize, saying, "Heaven has sent it to us;" so they treated the boy very kindly, and brought him up with such care that everyone liked and loved him.

Thirteen years passed, when the king came by chance to the mill, and seeing the boy, asked the miller if that was his son.

"No," said he, "I found him as a babe, floating down the river in a box into the mill-dam."

"How long ago?" asked the king.

"Some thirteen years," said the miller.

"He is a fine fellow," said the king. "Can you spare him to carry a letter to the queen? It will please me very much, and I will give him two pieces of gold for his trouble."

"As your majesty pleases," said the miller.

Now the king had guessed at once that this must be the child he had tried to drown, so he wrote a letter by him to the queen saying, "As soon as the bearer of this reaches you, let him be killed and buried so that all may be over before I come back."

The lad set out with this letter but missed his way, and came in the evening to a dark wood. Through the gloom he saw a far off light. He went towards it, and found that it came from a little cottage. There was no one in it except an old woman, who was frightened at seeing him, and said, "Why have you come here, and where are you going?"

"I am going to the queen, to whom I was to have given a letter; but I have lost my way, and shall be glad if you will give me a night's rest."

"You are very unlucky," said she, "for this is a robbers' hut; and if the band come back while you are here it may be worse for you."

"I am so tired," replied he, "that I must take my chance, for I can go no further." So he laid the letter on the table, stretched himself out upon a bench and fell asleep.

When the robbers came home and saw him, they asked the old

woman who the strange lad was. "I have given him shelter for charity," said she; "he had a letter to carry to the queen, and lost his way."

The robbers took up the letter, broke it open, and read the orders in it to murder the bearer. Then their leader was very angry at the king's trick, so he tore his letter, and wrote a fresh one, begging the queen, as soon as the young man reached her, to marry him to the princess. Meantime they let him sleep on till morning broke, and then showed him the right way to the queen's palace; where, as soon as she had read the letter, she made all ready for the wedding. As the young man was very handsome, the princess was very dutiful, and took him then and there for a husband.

After a while the king came back; and when he saw that this luck-child was married to the princess, in spite of all he had done to have him killed, he asked angrily how this had happened, and why his orders had not been obeyed.

"Dear husband," said the queen, "here is your letter – read it for yourself."

The king took it, and seeing that an exchange had been made, asked his son-in-law what he had done with the letter he gave him to carry.

"I know nothing of it," said he. "If it is not the one you gave me, it must have been taken away in the night, when I slept."

Then the king said fiercely, "No man shall have my daughter who does not go down into the magic cave and bring me three golden hairs from the beard of the giant king who reigns there. Do this, and you shall be my daughter's husband."

"I will soon do that," said the youth; so he took leave of his wife, and set out on his journey.

At the first city that he came to, the guard at the gate stopped him and asked what trade he followed, and what he knew.

"I know everything," said he.

"If that be so," said they, "you are just the man we want. Be so good as to find out why our fountain in the market-place is dry, and will give no water. Tell us the cause of that, and we will give you two asses laden with gold."

"With all my heart," said he, "when I come back."

Then he journeyed on, and came to another city, and there the guard also asked him what trade he followed, and what he knew.

"I know everything," said he.

"Then pray do us a good turn," said they. "Tell us why a tree, which always before bore us golden apples, does not even bear a leaf this year."

"Most willingly," said he, "when I come back."

At last his way led him to the side of a great lake of water, over which he must pass. The ferryman soon began to ask, as the others had done, what was his trade, and what he knew.

"Everything," said he.

"Then," said the other, "pray tell me why I am forced for ever to ferry over this water, and have never been able to get my freedom. I will reward you handsomely."

"Ferry me over," said the young man, "and I will tell you all about it as I come home."

When he had passed the water, he came to the magic cave. It looked very black and gloomy; but the wizard king was not at home, and his grandmother sat at the door in her easy chair.

"What do you want?" said she.

"Three golden hairs from the giant's beard," answered he.

"You will run a great risk," said she, "when he comes home; yet I will do what I can for you."

Then she changed him into an ant, and told him to hide himself in the folds of her cloak.

"Very well," said he; "but I want also to know why the city fountain is dry; why the tree that bore golden apples is now leafless; and what it is that binds the ferryman to his post."

"You seem fond of asking riddles," said the old dame, "but lie still, and listen to what the giant says when I pull the golden hairs, and perhaps you may learn what you want."

Soon night set in, and the old giant came home. As soon as he entered he began to sniff the air, and cried, "Something's wrong: I smell man's flesh."

Then he searched all round in vain, and the old dame scolded, and said, "Why turn everything topsy-turvy? I have just set all straight."

Upon this he laid his head in her lap, and soon fell asleep. As soon as he began to snore, she seized one of the golden hairs of his beard and pulled it out.

"Mercy!" cried he, starting up. "What are you doing?"

"I had a dream that woke me," said she, "and in my trouble I seized hold of your hair. I dreamt that the fountain in the market-place of the city had become dry, and would give no water; what can be the cause?"

"Ah! If they could find that out they would be glad," said the giant. "Under a stone in the fountain sits a toad; when they kill him, it will flow again."

Then he fell asleep again and the old lady pulled out another hair.

"What are you doing?" cried he in a rage.

"Don't be angry," said she, "I did it in my sleep. I dreamt that I was in a great kingdom a long way off, and that there was a beautiful tree there, that used to bear golden apples, but that now has not even a leaf upon it. What is the meaning of that?"

"Aha!" said the giant. "They would like to know that! At the root of the tree a mouse is gnawing; if they were to kill him, the tree would bear golden apples again; if not, it will soon die. Now do let me sleep in peace; if you wake me again, you shall rue it."

Then he fell asleep once more; and when she heard him snore she pulled out the third golden hair, and the giant jumped up and threatened her sorely; but she soothed him, and said, "It was a very strange dream I had this time. I thought I saw a ferryman, who was bound to ply backwards and forwards over a great lake, and could never find out how to set himself free. What is the charm that binds him?"

"A silly fool!" said the giant. "If he were to give the rudder into the hand of any passenger that came, he would find himself free, and the other would be forced to take his place. Now pray let me sleep."

In the morning the giant arose and went out; and the old woman gave the young man the three golden hairs, told him the three answers, and sent him on his way. He soon came to the ferryman, who knew him again, and asked for the promised answer.

"Ferry me over first," said he, "and then I will tell you."

When the boat reached the other side, he told him to give the rudder to the first passenger that came, and then he might run away as soon as he pleased.

The next place that he came to was the city where the barren tree stood.

"Kill the mouse," said he, "that is gnawing the tree's root, and you will have golden apples again."

They gave him a rich gift for this news, and he journeyed on to the city where the fountain had dried up. The guard asked him how to make the water flow. So he told them how to cure that mischief, and they thanked him, and gave him the two asses laden with gold.

And now at last this luckchild reached home, and his wife was very glad to see him and to hear how well everything had gone with him. Then he gave the three golden hairs to the King, who could no longer refuse to accept him as his son-in-law, though he was at heart quite as

189

spiteful against him as ever. The gold, however, astonished him, and when he saw all the treasure, he cried out with joy, "My dear son, where did you find all this gold?"

"By the side of a lake," said the youth, "where there is plenty more to be had."

"Pray tell me where it lies," said the king, "that I may go and get some too."

"As much as you please," replied the other. "You must set out and travel on and on, till you come to the shore of a great lake. There you will see a ferryman; let him carry you across, and when once you are over, you will see gold as plentiful as sand upon the shore."

Away went the greedy king. When he came to the lake he beckoned to the ferryman, who gladly took him into his boat, and as soon as he was there gave the rudder into his hand and sprang ashore, leaving the old king to ferry away, as a reward for his craftiness and treachery.

"And is his majesty plying there to this day?" You may be sure of that, for nobody will trouble himself to take the rudder out of his hands.

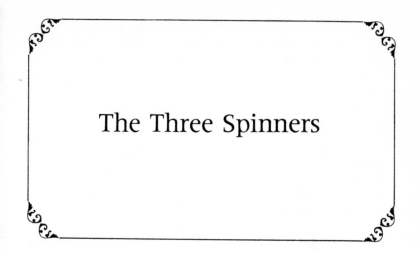

The Three Spinners

There was once a girl who was idle and would not spin, and however much her mother scolded her she still refused to do it. At last the mother lost all patience and beat her, at which the girl began to weep loudly.

Now at this very moment the Queen drove by, and when she heard the weeping she stopped her carriage, went into the house, and asked the mother why she was beating her daughter so that the cries could be heard out on the road. The woman was ashamed to reveal the laziness of her daughter and said, "I cannot get her to leave off spinning. She insists on spinning all day long, and I am poor, and cannot buy the flax."

"There is nothing I like better than spinning," said the Queen, "and I am never happier than when the wheels are humming. Let me have your daughter with me in the palace. I have plenty of flax, and there she shall spin as much as she likes."

The mother was delighted at this, and the Queen took the girl with her. When they arrived at the palace, she led her up into three rooms which were filled from top to bottom with the finest flax.

"Now spin me this flax," said she, "and when you have done it, you shall have my eldest son for a husband, even though you are poor. I care nothing for that; your wonderful industry is dowry enough."

The girl was secretly terrified, for she could not have spun the flax, no, not if she had lived till she was three hundred years old, and had sat at it every day from morning till night. When she was left alone she began to weep and sat thus for three days without moving a finger. On the third day the Queen came, and when she saw that nothing had been spun yet, she was surprised; but the girl excused herself by saying that she had not been able to begin because of her great distress at leaving her mother's house. The Queen was satisfied with this, but said, "Tomorrow you must begin to work."

When the girl was alone again, she did not know what to do, and in her distress went to the window. Then she saw three women coming towards her, the first of whom had a broad flat foot, the second had such a great underlip that it hung down over her chin, and the third had a broad thumb. They stood outside the window, looked up, and asked the girl what was amiss.

She told them of her trouble, and they offered her their help and said, "If you will invite us to the wedding, not be ashamed of us, call us your aunts, and place us at your table, we will spin the flax for you in a very short time."

"With all my heart," she replied. "Do come in and begin the work at once."

Then she let in the three strange women, and cleared a place in the first room, where they seated themselves and began their spinning. One drew the thread and trod the wheel, the next wetted the thread, the third twisted it and struck the table with her finger, and as often as she struck it, a skein of thread fell to the ground, spun in the finest manner possible. The girl concealed the three spinners from the Queen, and showed her whenever she came the great quantity of spun thread. The Queen was full of praise for her. When the first room was empty she went to the second, and at last to the third, and that too was quickly cleared. Then the three women took their leave and said to the girl, "Do not forget what you have promised us – it will make your fortune."

When the Queen was shown the empty rooms, and the great heap of yarn, she gave orders for the wedding, and the bridegroom rejoiced that he was to have such a clever and industrious wife, and praised her mightily.

"I have three aunts," said the girl, "and as they have been very kind to me, I should not like to forget them in my good fortune. May I please invite them to the wedding and let them sit with us at table?"

The Queen and the bridegroom said, "Why should we not allow that?"

So when the feast began, the three women entered in strange apparel, and the bride said, "Welcome, dear aunts."

"Ah," said the bridegroom, "how come you by these hideous friends?" Thereupon he went to the one with the broad flat foot and said, "How do you come by such a broad flat foot?"

"By treading the spinning-wheel," she answered.

Then the bridegroom went to the second and said, "How do you come by your wide lips?"

"By licking the thread," she answered.

Then he asked the third, "How do you come by your broad thumb?"

"By twisting the thread," she answered.

At this the King's son was alarmed and said, "Never shall my beautiful bride touch a spinning-wheel."

And so she was free for ever of the hateful flax-spinning.

The White Snake

A long time ago there lived a king who was famed for his wisdom throughout all the land. But he had an odd habit: every day after dinner, when the table was cleared, and no one else was present, a trusty servant had to bring him one more dish. It was covered, however, and even the servant did not know what was in it, for the King never took off the cover until he was quite alone.

One day the servant was overcome with such curiosity that he could not help carrying the dish into his own room. When he had carefully locked the door, he lifted the cover, and saw a white snake lying on the dish. He could not resist tasting it, so he cut off a little bit and put it into his mouth. No sooner had it touched his tongue than he heard a strange whispering of little voices outside his window. He listened, and then realized that it was the sparrows who were chattering together, and telling one another of all kinds of things which they had seen in the fields and woods. Eating the snake had given him the power of understanding the language of animals.

Now it so happened that on this very day the Queen lost her most beautiful ring, and suspicion of having stolen it fell upon this trusty servant, who was allowed to go everywhere. The King sent for him, and threatened with angry words that unless by the next day he could

195

prove that someone else was the thief, he would be executed. In vain he declared his innocence; he was not believed.

In his trouble and fear he went down into the courtyard to think how he could get out of his difficulty. Some ducks were sitting quietly by a brook, and while they smoothed their feathers with their bills, they quacked confidentially together. The servant stood by and listened. They were telling one another of all the places where they had been waddling about all the morning, and what good food they had found. Then one said fretfully, "Something lies heavy on my stomach; as I was eating in haste I swallowed a ring which lay under the Queen's window."

The servant at once seized her by the neck, carried her into the kitchen, and said to the cook, "Here's a fine duck; pray kill her."

"Yes," said the cook, and weighed her in his hand; "she has spared no trouble to fatten herself, and it's high time she was roasted." So he killed her, and when he cut her open, the Queen's ring was found inside her.

The servant could now easily prove his innocence; and the King, to make amends for the wrong, promised him the best place in the court that he could wish for. The servant refused everything, except a horse and some money, as he had a mind to travel and see the world.

When his request was granted he set out on his way, and one day came to a pond, where he saw three fishes caught in the reeds and gasping for water. As he had a kind heart, he got off his horse and put the three prisoners back into the water. They quivered with delight, put out their heads, and cried to him, "We'll remember you and repay you for saving us!"

He rode on, and after a while he seemed to hear a voice in the sand at his feet. He listened, and heard an ant-king complain, "Why cannot folks, with their clumsy beasts, keep off our bodies? That stupid horse with his heavy hooves has trodden on some of my people in the most heartless way!" So he turned on to a side path to avoid the ants and the ant-king cried out to him, "We'll remember you – one good turn deserves another!"

The path led him into a wood, and there he saw two old ravens standing by their nest, and throwing out their young ones.

"Out with you, you idle, good-for-nothing creatures!" cried they. "We can't find food for you any longer; you are big enough to provide for yourselves."

The poor young ravens lay on the ground flapping their wings, and crying, "Oh, what helpless nestlings we are! We must shift for ourselves, and yet we can't even fly! What can we do, but lie here and starve?"

So the good young fellow alighted and killed his horse with his sword, and gave it to them for food. They came hopping up to it, satisfied their hunger, and cried, "We'll remember you – one good turn deserves another!"

And now he had to use his own legs, and when he had walked a long way, he came to a large city. There was a great noise and crowd in the streets, and a man rode up on horseback, crying aloud, "The King's daughter wants a husband; but whoever sues for her hand must perform a hard task, and if he does not succeed he will forfeit his life." Many had already made the attempt, but in vain; nevertheless when the youth saw the King's daughter he was so overcome by her great beauty that he forgot all danger, went to the King, and declared himself a suitor.

So he was led out to the sea, and a gold ring was thrown into it. Then the King ordered him to fetch the ring up from the bottom of the sea, and added, "If you come up without it you will be thrown in again and again until you perish amid the waves." All the people grieved for the handsome youth; then they went away, leaving him alone by the sea.

He stood on the shore and considered what to do, when suddenly he saw three fishes swimming towards him. They were the very fishes whose lives he had saved! The one in the middle held a mussel in its mouth, which it laid on the shore at the youth's feet, and when he had taken it up and opened it, there lay the gold ring in the shell. Full of joy he took it to the King, expecting the promised reward.

But when the proud princess saw that he was not her equal in birth, she scorned him, and required him to perform another task. She went down into the garden and strewed with her own hands ten sacksful of millet seed on the grass. "Tomorrow," she said, "before sunrise these must be picked up – every single one."

197

The youth sat down in the garden, wondering how he could possibly perform this task, but he could think of nothing. There he sat sorrowfully awaiting the break of day, when he would be led to death. But as soon as the first rays of the sun shone into the garden he saw all the ten sacks standing side by side, quite full, and not a single grain was missing. The ant-king had come in the night with thousands and thousands of ants, and the grateful creatures had picked up all the millet seed and gathered it into the sacks.

Presently the King's daughter herself came down into the garden, and was amazed to see the young man had done the task she had set him. But she could not yet conquer her proud heart, and said, "Although he has performed both the tasks, he shall not be my husband until he has brought me an apple from the Tree of Life."

The youth did not know where the Tree of Life stood, but he set out, and would have gone on as long as his legs would carry him, though he had no hope of finding it. After he had wandered through three kingdoms, he came one evening to a wood, and lay down under a tree to sleep. But he heard a rustling in the branches, and a golden apple fell into his hand. At the same time three ravens flew down, perched upon his knee, and said, "We are the three young ravens whom you saved from starving. When we had grown big, and heard that you were seeking the Golden Apple, we flew over the sea to the end of the world, where the Tree of Life stands, and have brought you the apple."

The youth, full of joy, set out homewards, and took the Golden Apple to the King's beautiful daughter, who had now no more excuses left to make. They cut the Apple of Life in two and ate it together; and then her heart became full of love for him, and they lived happily to a great age.

The
Poor Miller's Boy
and the Cat

There once was an old miller who had neither wife nor child. Three apprentices served under him in his mill. When they had been with him several years, he said to them one day, "I am old, and want only to sit in the chimney corner. Go into the world, and whichever of you brings me the best horse, to him will I give the mill, and in return for it he shall take care of me till my death."

Two of the boys thought the third boy was a simpleton, and made him do all the menial work. They begrudged him the mill, and determined he should not have it. All three set out together, and when they came to the village, the two said to stupid Hans, "You may just as well stay here, for as long as you live you'll never get a horse."

Hans, however, went with them, and when it was night they came to a cave in which they lay down to sleep. The two bright boys waited until Hans had fallen asleep; then they got up, and went away leaving him where he was. They thought they had done a very clever thing, but they were wrong.

When the sun rose, and Hans woke up, he was lying in a deep cavern. He looked around and exclaimed, "Oh, heavens, where am I?" Then he got up, clambered out of the cave, went into the forest and thought, "Here I am quite alone and deserted. How can I get a horse?"

While he was walking along deep in thought, he met a small tabby cat. "Where are you going, Hans?" she asked him in a kind voice.

"Alas, you cannot help me."

"I know what you seek," said the cat. "You are looking for a beautiful horse. Come with me, and be my faithful servant for seven years, and then I'll give you a horse more beautiful than any you have ever seen in your whole life."

"Well, this is a wonderful cat!" thought Hans. "But I must make sure she is telling the truth."

She took him with her into her enchanted castle, where there were nothing but cats who were her servants. They leapt nimbly upstairs and downstairs, and were merry and happy. In the evening when they sat down to dinner, three of them had to make music. One played the bassoon, the second the fiddle, and the third put the trumpet to his lips, and blew till his cheeks ballooned out. After dinner the table was carried away, and the cat said, "Now, Hans, come and dance with me."

"No," said he, "I won't dance with a pussy cat. I've never done that yet."

"Then take him to bed," said she to the other cats. So one of them lighted him to his bedroom, one pulled his shoes off, one his stockings, and at last one of them blew out the candle.

Next morning they returned and helped him out of bed; one put his stockings on for him, and one dried his face with her tail.

"That feels very soft!" said Hans. He, however, had to serve the cat, and chop some wood every day, and to do that he had an axe of silver. The wedge and saw were of silver too, and the mallet of copper. He chopped the wood well, stayed there in the castle and had good meat and drink, but never saw anyone but the tabby cat and her servants.

One day she said to him, "Go and mow my meadow and dry the grass." She gave him a scythe of silver, and a whetstone of gold, but bade him deliver them up again carefully. So Hans did what he was bidden, and when he had finished the work, he carried the scythe, whetstone and hay to the house, and asked if it was not yet time for his reward.

"No," said the cat, "you must first do something else for me. You will find here timber, carpenter's axe, square, and everything that is needful, all made of silver. With these build me a small house."

Hans built the small house, and said that he had now done everything she asked, and still he had no horse. Meanwhile the seven years had gone by for him as if they were six months. The cat asked if he would like to see her horses.

"Yes," said Hans.

Then she opened the door of the small house, and there stood twelve horses – horses so well-groomed and shining that his heart rejoiced at the sight of them.

And now the cat gave him food and drink, and said, "Go home. I won't give you your horse to take with you; but in three days I will follow you and bring it."

So Hans set out, and the cat showed him the way to the mill. She had, however, never once given him a new coat, and he had been obliged to wear his dirty old smock, which he had brought with him, and which during the seven years had everywhere become too small for him. When he reached home, the two other apprentices were there already, and each of them certainly had brought a horse with him, but one of them was blind, and the other lame. They asked Hans where his horse was.

"It will follow me in three days' time."

They laughed and said, "Stupid Hans! Where would the likes of you get a horse?"

Hans went into the parlour, but the miller said he could not sit down to table, for he was so ragged and torn that they would all be ashamed of him if anyone came in. So they gave him a mouthful of food outside, and at night the two others would not let Hans have a bed, and he was forced to creep into the goose-house, and lie down on a little hard straw.

In the morning the three days had passed, and a coach came with six horses. Their coats shone so brightly that it was a delight to see them! A servant brought a seventh as well, which was for the poor miller's boy. And a magnificent princess alighted from the coach and went into the mill, and this princess was the little tabby cat whom poor

Hans had served for seven years. She asked the miller where the miller's boy was.

"He is lying in the goose-house," the miller said. "We cannot have him in the mill, for he is so ragged."

Then the King's daughter said that they were to bring him immediately. So they fetched him, and he had to hold his outgrown smock together to cover himself. The servants unpacked splendid garments, and washed him, and dressed him, and when that was done, no King could have looked more handsome. Then the princess asked to see the horses which the other apprentices had brought home with them – the one blind, the other lame. She ordered a servant to bring the seventh horse, and when the miller saw it, he said that such a horse had never before entered his yard.

"That one was brought by the third miller's boy," said she

"Then he must have the mill," said the miller, but the King's daughter said that the miller had got the horse, and he could keep his mill as well. She took her faithful Hans with her in the coach, and drove away. They went first to the little house which he had built with the silver tools, and behold, it was a great castle! Everything inside it was of silver and gold. And then she married him, and he was rich, so rich that he had enough for all the rest of his life.

After this, let no one say that anyone who is silly can never become a person of importance.

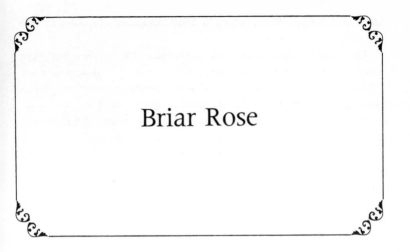

Briar Rose

A long time ago there lived a King and Queen who said every day, "Ah, if only we had a child!" but they never had one. But it happened that once when the Queen was bathing, a frog crept out of the water, and said to her, "Your wish shall be fulfilled; before a year has gone by you shall have a daughter."

What the frog had said came true, and the Queen had a little girl who was so pretty that the King could not contain himself for joy, and ordered a great feast. He invited not only his relations, friends and acquaintances, but also the fairies, in order that they might be kind and well-disposed towards the child. There were thirteen of them in his kingdom, but, as he had only twelve golden plates for them to eat off, one of them had to stay at home.

The feast was held with all splendour, and when it came to an end the fairies bestowed their magic gifts upon the baby. One gave virtue, another beauty, a third riches, and so on – everything in the world that one could wish for.

When eleven of them had made their promises, suddenly the thirteenth came in. She wished to avenge herself for not having been invited, and without greeting, she cried in a loud voice, "The King's daughter shall in her fifteenth year prick herself with a spindle and fall down dead." And without saying a word more she turned and left the room.

They were all shocked; but the twelfth fairy, whose good wish was still unspoken, came forward. She could not undo the evil sentence, but only soften it, so she said, "It shall not be death, but a deep sleep of a hundred years, into which the princess shall fall."

The King was so anxious to keep his dear child from misfortune that he gave orders that every spindle in the kingdom should be burnt.

As time went by the promises of the fairies all came true. The princess was so beautiful, modest, good-natured, and wise, that everyone who saw her loved her.

Now it happened that on the very day when she was fifteen years old, the King and Queen were not at home, and the maiden was left in the palace quite alone. She wandered about the palace, and at last came to an old tower. She climbed up the narrow winding staircase, and reached a little door. A rusty key was in the lock, and when she turned it the door sprang open, and there in a little room sat an old woman with a spindle, busily spinning her flax.

"Good day, old dame," said the King's daughter. "What are you doing there?"

"I am spinning," said the old woman, and nodded her head.

"What sort of thing is that, that rattles round so merrily?" said the girl, and she took the spindle and wanted to spin too. But scarcely had she touched the spindle when the magic decree was fulfilled, and she pricked her finger with it. And, at that very moment, she fell down upon the bed that stood there, and lay in a deep sleep. And this sleep extended over the whole palace: the King and Queen who had just come home, and had entered the great hall, began to go to sleep, and the whole of the court with them. The horses, too, went to sleep in the stable, the dogs in the yard, the pigeons upon the roof, the flies on the wall: even the fire that was flaming on the hearth became quiet and slept, the roast meat left off sizzling, and the cook, who was just going to pull the hair of the scullery boy, because he had forgotten something, let him go, and went to sleep. And the wind fell, and on the trees before the castle not a leaf moved again.

Round about the castle there began to grow a hedge of briar roses.

Every year it grew higher, till at last it surrounded the castle and completely covered it, so that there was nothing of it to be seen, not even the flag upon the roof. But the story of the beautiful sleeping Briar Rose, for so the princess was named, spread far and wide, so that from time to time princes came and tried to get through the thorny hedge into the castle.

But they found it impossible, for the thorns held them fast.

After long, long years a prince came again to that country, and heard an old man talking about the thorn hedge. He said that a castle was said to stand behind it in which a most beautiful princess, called Briar Rose, had been asleep for a hundred years; and that the King and Queen and the whole court were asleep too. He had heard from his grandfather that many princes had already tried to get through the thorny hedge, but they had been caught in it, and had died a sad death. Then the youth said, "I am not afraid. I will go and see beautiful Briar Rose." The old man tried to dissuade him but he would not listen.

By this time the hundred years had passed, and the day had come when Briar Rose was to wake up again. When the prince came near to the thorn hedge, it was covered in beautiful flowers, which of their own accord, let him pass unhurt, then closed again behind him like a hedge. In the castle yard he saw the horses and the spotted hounds lying asleep; on the roof sat the pigeons with their heads under their wings. And when he entered the house, the flies were asleep upon the wall, the cook in the kitchen was still holding out his hand to seize the boy, and the maid was sitting by the black hen which she was going to pluck. In the great hall he saw the whole of the court lying asleep, and by the throne lay the King and Queen.

Then he went on still further, and all was so quiet that he could hear his own breathing. At last he came to the tower, and opened the door into the little room where Briar Rose was sleeping. There she lay, so beautiful that he could not turn his eyes away; and he stooped down and gave her a kiss. At once Briar Rose opened her eyes, and looked at him lovingly.

Then they went down together, and the King awoke, and the Queen, and the whole court, and looked at each other in great astonishment. The horses in the courtyard stood up and shook themselves; the hounds jumped up and wagged their tails; the pigeons upon the roof took their heads from under their wings, looked round, and flew into the open country; the flies on the wall began to walk again; the fire in the kitchen burned up and flickered and cooked the meat; the joint began to turn and sizzle again; the cook gave the boy such a box on the ear that he screamed, and the maid plucked the fowl ready for roasting.

Then the marriage of the prince with Briar Rose was celebrated with great splendour, and they lived happily to the end of their days.

The Singing, Soaring Lark

There was once upon a time a man who was about to set out on a long journey, so he asked his three daughters what he should bring back for them. The eldest asked for pearls, the second diamonds, but the third said, "Dear Father, I should like a singing, soaring lark." The father said, "Yes, if I can get it, you shall have it," kissed all three, and set out.

Now when he was on his way home again, he brought pearls and diamonds for the two eldest, but he had sought everywhere in vain for a singing, soaring lark for the youngest, and he was very unhappy about it, for she was his favourite child.

His road lay through a forest, and in the midst of it was a splendid castle, and near the castle stood a tree, and right on the top of the tree he saw a singing, soaring lark.

"Aha, you come just at the right moment!" he said, delighted, and called to his servant to climb up and catch it. But as he approached the tree, a lion leapt from beneath it, shook himself, and roared till the leaves on the trees trembled. "He who tries to steal my singing, soaring lark," he cried, "will I devour."

Then the man said, "I had no idea that the bird belonged to you. I will make amends for the wrong I have done and pay you a large sum of money, if only you will spare my life."

"Nothing can save you," the lion said, "unless you promise to give

209

me what meets you first on your return home. If you will do that, I will grant you your life, and you shall have the bird for your daughter into the bargain."

The man hesitated, and said, "That might mean giving my youngest daughter. She loves me best, and always runs to meet me on my return home."

The servant, however, was terrified of the lion, and said, "Why should your daughter be the very one to meet you? It might easily be a cat or dog."

So the man allowed himself to be persuaded, took the singing, soaring lark, and promised to give the lion whatever should first meet him on his return home.

When he reached home and entered the house, the first who met him was his youngest and dearest daughter, who came running up, kissed and embraced him. When she saw that he had brought with him a singing, soaring lark, she was beside herself with joy.

Her father, however, began to weep, and said, "My darling child, I have paid dearly for the little bird. In return for it I have been obliged to promise you to a savage lion, who will tear you in pieces and devour you." He told her all that had happened, and begged her not to go to the lion, come what might. But she consoled him, and said, "Dearest father, you must keep your promise. But I will go and entreat the lion to let me come safely back to you."

Next morning she went fearlessly out into the forest. The lion, however, was a prince under a spell. By day he and all his people were lions, but in the night they resumed their human shapes.

On the maiden's arrival she was kindly received and led into the castle. When night came, the lion turned into a handsome prince, and their wedding was celebrated with great magnificence. They lived happily together, remained awake at night, and slept in the daytime.

One day the lion prince said, "Tomorrow there is a feast in your father's house, because your eldest sister is to be married. If you want to go to it, my lions shall conduct you."

She said, "Yes, I should dearly like to see my father again," and set off, accompanied by the lions. There was great joy when she arrived, for they had all believed that she had been torn in pieces and killed by

210

the lion. But she told them what a handsome husband she had, and how well off she was. She remained with them while the wedding feast lasted, and then went back to the forest.

When the second daughter was about to be married, and the princess was again invited to the wedding, she said to the lion, "This time you must come with me." The lion, however, said that was too dangerous for him, for if when there a ray from a burning candle fell on him, he would be changed into a dove for seven years. She said, "Ah, but do come with me. I will take great care of you, and guard you from all light."

So they went away together, and took their little child as well. The girl had a chamber built in her father's house, so strong and thick that no ray could pierce through it; in this the lion was to shut himself up when the candles were lit for the wedding feast. But the door was made of green wood which warped and left a little crack which no one noticed. When the wedding procession with all its candles and torches came back from church, and passed by this apartment, a ray about the breadth of a hair fell on the prince, and he was transformed in an instant into a white dove. The dove said to the girl, "For seven years must I fly about the world, but at every seventh step you take I will let fall a drop of red blood and a white feather. These will show you the way, and if you follow the trail you can release me." Then the dove flew out at the door, and she followed him, and at every seventh step a red drop of blood and a little white feather fell down and showed her the way.

She journeyed continually about in the wide world, following the prince. When the seven years were almost passed she rejoiced to think their cares would soon be over. But this was not to be. Once at her seventh step no little feather and no drop of red blood fell, and when she raised her eyes the dove had disappeared. "In this no man can help us," she thought, and so she climbed up to the sun, and said to him, "You shine into every crevice, and over every peak. Have you seen a white dove flying?"

"No," said the sun, "I have seen none, but here is a casket. Open it when you are in sorest need."

The girl thanked the sun, and went on until evening came and the

211

moon appeared. She asked the moon, "You shine on every field and forest. Have you seen a white dove flying ?"

"No," said the moon, "I have seen no white dove, but here is an egg. Break it when you are in great need."

She thanked the moon, and went on until the night wind blew on her. She said to it, "You blow over every tree and under every leaf. Have you seen a white dove flying ?"

"No," said the night wind, "I have seen none, but I will ask the three other winds. Perhaps they have seen it."

The east wind and the west wind came, and they had seen nothing, but the south wind said, "I have seen the white dove. It has flown to the Red Sea. There it has become a lion again, for the seven years are over. The lion is fighting with a dragon; the dragon, however, is an enchanted princess."

The night wind said, "Go to the Red Sea. On the right bank are some tall reeds. Count them, break off the eleventh, and strike the dragon with it. Then the lion will be able to subdue it, and both will regain their human form. After that, look for the griffin which is by the Red Sea. Leap with your beloved on his back, and the bird will carry you over the sea to your own home. Here is a nut. When you are above the centre of the sea, let the nut fall; it will immediately shoot up, and a tall nut-tree will grow out of the water. On this the griffin may rest; for if he cannot rest, he will not be strong enough to carry you across."

The girl found everything as the night wind had said. She counted the reeds by the sea, cut off the eleventh, and struck the dragon with it. The lion overcame it, and immediately he and the princess regained their human shapes. But when the princess, who had before been the dragon, was delivered from enchantment, she seated herself on the griffin, and carried the prince off with her.

There stood the poor girl who had wandered so far and was again forsaken. She sat down and cried, but at last she took courage and said, "I will go as far as the wind blows, and as long as the cock crows, until I find him." She walked by long, long roads, until at last she came to the castle where the prince and the princess were living. She heard that soon a feast was to be held to celebrate their wedding. She opened the casket that the sun had given her. In it lay a dress as brilliant as the sun

itself. She took it out and put it on, and went up into the castle, and everyone, even the bride herself, looked at her with astonishment. The dress pleased the bride so well that she wanted it for her wedding-dress, and asked if it was for sale.

"Not for money or land," answered the girl. "But let me sleep one night in the room where the bridegroom sleeps."

The bride wanted very much to have the dress; so at last she consented, but the page was to give the prince a sleeping draught. When it was night, and the prince was asleep, the girl was led into the chamber; she seated herself on the bed, and said, "I have followed you for seven years. I have been to the sun and the moon, and the four winds, seeking you, and helped you to overcome the dragon. How can you forget me?"

But the prince slept so soundly that it only seemed to him as if the wind were whistling outside in the fir trees. When day broke, the girl was led out again, and had to give up the golden dress. She went out into a meadow and sat down, and wept. Then she thought of the egg which the moon had given her; she opened it, and there came out a clucking hen with twelve chicks all of gold. They ran about cheeping, and crept again under the hen's wings; nothing more beautiful was ever seen in the world! The girl drove them through the meadow before her, to the bride's window. She immediately came down and asked if the golden chicks were for sale.

"Not for money or land," said the girl, "but let me sleep another night in the chamber where the bridegroom sleeps."

The bride said, "Yes," intending to cheat her as on the former evening. But when the prince went to bed he asked the page what the murmuring and rustling in the night had been. At this the page told all; that he had been forced to give him a sleeping draught, because a poor girl had slept secretly in the chamber, and that he was to give him another that night. The prince said, "Pour away the draught."

At night, the girl was again led in, and when she began to relate how ill all had fared with her, he immediately recognized his beloved wife by her voice, sprang up and cried, "Now I really am released! I have been in a dream, for the strange princess bewitched me so that I was compelled to forget you, but now the spell is broken!"

knock, but the knock was at the door of his room. It was his neighbour, a poor man who had no food for his children.

"I know," thought the poor man, "that my neighbour is rich, but he is as hard as he is rich. I don't believe he will help me, but my children are crying for bread, so I will venture it." He said to the rich man, "I am desperate. My children are starving. Lend me four measures of corn."

The rich man looked at him long, and then the first sunbeam of mercy began to melt away some of the ice of his greediness. "I won't lend you four measures," he answered, "but I will make you a present of eight, but you must fulfil one condition."

"What am I to do?" said the poor man.

"When I am dead, watch for three nights by my grave."

The peasant was disturbed at the request, but he was so poor he would have consented to anything; so he accepted, and carried the corn home with him.

It seemed as if the rich man had foreseen what was about to happen; for three days later he suddenly dropped dead. No one grieved for him. When he was buried, the poor man remembered his promise; he would willingly have been released from it, but thought, "After all, he acted kindly by me. I have fed my hungry children with his corn, and I must keep my promise." At nightfall he went into the churchyard, and sat on the grave-mound. Everything was quiet; the moon appeared above the grave, and an owl flew past and uttered her melancholy cry. When the sun rose, the poor man went safely home, and in the same manner the second night passed. On the evening of the third day he felt a strange uneasiness. It seemed to him that something was about to happen. When he went out he saw, by the churchyard wall, a man whom he had never seen before. He was no longer young, had scars on his face, and his eyes looked sharply round. He was covered with an old cloak: nothing was visible but his great riding boots.

"What are you looking for here?" the peasant asked. "Aren't you afraid of this lonely place?"

"I'm looking for nothing," he answered, "and I'm afraid of nothing! I'm only a paid-off soldier, and I mean to pass the night here, because I have no other shelter."

"If you are without fear," said the peasant, "stay with me and help me watch that grave there."

"To keep watch is a soldier's business," he replied. "Whatever happens here, whether good or bad, we'll share it between us."

The peasant agreed, and they seated themselves on the grave together. All was quiet until midnight, when suddenly a shrill whistling was heard, and the two watchers saw the Evil One standing before them.

"Be off, you ragamuffins!" cried he. "The man who lies in that grave belongs to me. I want to take him, and if you don't go away I'll wring your necks!"

"Sir with the red cloak," said the soldier, "you are not my captain; I've no need to obey you, and I've not yet learned how to fear. Go away. We shall stay here."

The Devil thought to himself, "Money is the best thing with which to bribe these two vagabonds." So he asked quite kindly if they would accept a bag of money, and go home with it.

"Now you're talking," answered the soldier, "but one bag of gold won't serve us. If you will give us as much as will go into one of my boots, we'll go away."

218

"I haven't so much as that about me," said the Devil, "but I will fetch it. In the next town lives a money-changer who is a good friend of mine, and who will readily advance it to me."

When the Devil had vanished the soldier took his left boot off, and said, "We'll soon get the better of that fellow. Just give me your knife, comrade." He cut the sole off the boot, and put it in the high grass near the grave on the edge of a hole that was half overgrown. "That will do," said he; "now the rogue may come."

They waited, and it was not long before the Devil returned with a small bag of gold in his hand.

"Just pour it in," said the soldier, raising the boot a little, "but that won't be enough."

The Black One shook out all that was in the bag; the gold fell through, and the boot remained empty.

"You fool!" cried the soldier. "I told you it wasn't enough. Go back again, and bring more."

The Devil shook his head, went, and in an hour's time came with a much larger bag under his arm.

"Now pour it in," cried the soldier, "but I doubt if it will fill the boot!"

The gold clinked as it fell, but the boot remained empty.

"You have shamefully big calves to your legs!" cried the Devil, and made a wry face.

"Did you think," said the soldier, "that I had a cloven foot like you? Since when have you been so stingy? See that you get more gold together, or our bargain will come to nothing!"

The Wicked One went off again. This time he stayed away longer, and when at length he appeared he was panting under the weight of a sack on his shoulders. He emptied it into the boot, which was just as far from being filled as before. He was furious, and was just going to tear the boot out of the soldier's hands, when the first ray of the rising sun broke from the sky, and the Evil Spirit fled away with loud shrieks, so the poor soul was saved.

The peasant wanted to divide the gold, but the soldier said, "Give my share to the poor. I'll come with you to your cottage and together we'll live in peace on what remains."

One-eye, Two-eyes, and Three-eyes

There was once a woman who had three daughters. The eldest was called One-eye, because she had only one eye in the middle of her forehead, and the second Two-eyes, because she had two eyes like other folks, and the youngest, Three-eyes, because she had three eyes, the third also in the centre of her forehead. However, as Two-eyes saw just as other human beings did, her sisters and her mother could not endure her. They said, "You with your two eyes, are no better than the common people; you don't belong here!" They pushed her about, and made her wear old clothes and gave her nothing to eat but what they left, and did everything they could to make her unhappy.

One day Two-eyes had to go into the fields and tend the goat, but she was hungry, because her sisters had given her so little to eat. So she sat down and began to weep, so bitterly that two streams ran down from her eyes. She looked up – a woman was standing beside her, who said, "Why are you weeping, little Two-eyes?"

Two-eyes answered, "Have I not reason to weep, when I have two eyes like other people, and my sisters and mother hate me for it, and push me about, make me wear old clothes, and give me nothing to eat but the scraps they leave? Today they've given me so little that I'm still hungry."

Then the wise woman said, "Dry your tears, Two-eyes, and I'll tell

220

you something to stop you ever feeling hungry again. Just say to your goat,

> *'Bleat, my little goat, bleat,*
> *Cover the table with something to eat,'*

and a well-spread table will stand before you, with delicious food upon it. Eat as much of it as you want, and when you have had enough, just say,

> *'Bleat, my little goat, I pray,*
> *And take the table quite away.'*

and it will vanish."

Then the wise woman departed. But Two-eyes thought, "I must see if what she said is true, for I'm very hungry," and she said,

> *"Bleat, my little goat, bleat,*
> *Cover the table with something to eat."*

Scarcely had she spoken the words than a little table, covered with a white cloth, was standing there. On it were a plate, a knife and fork, a silver spoon, and the most delicious food, hot and steaming. Two-eyes helped herself to some food, and enjoyed it. And when she was satisfied, she said, as the wise woman had taught her,

> *"Bleat, my little goat, I pray,*
> *And take the table quite away,"*

and immediately the table and everything on it was gone again. "That is a delightful way of keeping house!" thought Two-eyes, and was very happy.

In the evening, when she went home with her goat, she found a small earthenware dish with some food, which her sisters had set ready for her, but she did not touch it. Next day she again went out with her goat, and left untouched the few bits of broken bread which had been handed to her. The first and second time that she did this, her sisters did not notice, but as it happened every time, they at last said, "There's something wrong about Two-eyes; she always leaves her food untasted, and she used to eat up everything we gave her; she must have discovered other ways of getting food."

So they resolved to send One-eye with Two-eyes when she went to drive her goat to the pasture, to see what Two-eyes did when she was there, and whether anyone brought her anything to eat and drink. One-eye said, "I'll go with you to the pasture, and see that the goat is cared for properly, and driven where there is food." But Two-eyes knew what was in One-eye's mind, and drove the goat into high grass and said, "Come, One-eye, we'll sit down, and I'll sing something to you." One-eye sat down, tired with the unaccustomed walk and the heat of the sun, and Two-eyes sang, "One-eye, are you awake? One-eye, are you asleep?" until One-eye shut her one eye, and fell asleep. As soon as Two-eyes saw that One-eye was fast asleep, and could see nothing, she said,

> "Bleat, my little goat, bleat,
> Cover the table with something to eat."

Then she sat at her table, and ate and drank until she was satisfied, and then she again cried,

> "Bleat, my little goat, I pray,
> And take the table quite away,"

and in an instant all was gone. Two-eyes now awakened One-eye, and said, "One-eye, dropping off to sleep is no way to take care of the goat. Why, it might have run half way round the world! Come, let's go home." So they went home, and again Two-eyes left her food untouched, and One-eye could not tell her mother why she would not eat it, and to excuse herself said, "I fell asleep when I was out."

Next day the mother said to Three-eyes, "This time you go and watch if Two-eyes eats anything when she is out, and if anyone brings her food and drink, for she must eat and drink in secret." So Three-eyes went to Two-eyes, and said, "I'll go with you and see if the goat is cared for properly, and driven where there is food." But Two-eyes knew what was in Three-eyes' mind, and drove the goat into high grass and said, "We'll sit down, and I'll sing something to you, Three-eyes." Three-eyes sat down, tired with the walk and with the heat of the sun, and Two-eyes sang, "Three-eyes, are you awake?" but then, instead of singing "Three-eyes, are you asleep?" as she meant to do, she thoughtlessly

222

sang, "Two-eyes, are you asleep?" and she went on singing, "Three-eyes, are you awake? Two-eyes, are you asleep?" Then two of Three-eyes' eyes shut and fell asleep, but the third, as it had not been named in the song, did not sleep. It is true that Three-eyes shut it, but only in her cunning, to pretend it was asleep too, but it blinked, and could see everything very well. And when Two-eyes thought that Three-eyes was fast asleep, she said,

> "Bleat, my little goat, bleat,
> Cover the table with something to eat."

She ate and drank as much as her heart desired, and then said,

> "Bleat, my little goat, I pray,
> And take the table quite away."

Three-eyes had seen everything. Then Two-eyes came to her, waked her and said, "Have you been asleep, Three-eyes? You are not much of a goatherd! Come, we'll go home." When they got home, Two-eyes again did not eat, and Three-eyes said to the mother, "Now I know why that stuck-up thing there doesn't eat. When she's out, she says to the goat,

> 'Bleat, my little goat, bleat,
> Cover the table with something to eat,'

and a little table appears before her covered with the best of food, much better than any we have here, and when she has eaten all she wants, she says,

> 'Bleat, my little goat, I pray,
> And take the table quite away,'

and it disappears. I watched everything closely. She put two of my eyes to sleep by a magic charm, but luckily the one nearest to her kept awake."

Then the jealous mother cried, "Why should she eat better food than we do? I'll soon put a stop to that!' and she fetched a butcher's knife and thrust it into the heart of the goat, which fell down dead.

When Two-eyes saw this, she went out full of trouble, sat in the field,

224

and wept bitter tears. Suddenly the wise woman once more stood by her side, and said, "Two-eyes, why are you weeping?"

"Have I not reason to weep?" she answered. "The goat which brought the table for me every day when I spoke your charm has been killed by my mother, and now I shall again have to bear hunger and want."

"Two-eyes," said the wise woman, "I will give you a piece of good advice: ask your sisters to give you the heart of the slaughtered goat. Bury it in front of the house, and your fortune will be made."

She vanished, and Two-eyes went home and said to her sisters, "Dear sisters, give me some part of my goat: not the best meat but just the heart."

They laughed and said, "If that's all you want, you can have it." So Two-eyes took the heart and buried it quietly in the evening, in front of the house-door, as the wise woman had counselled her to do.

Next morning outside the house-door stood a magnificent tree with leaves of silver and fruits of gold. In all the wide world there was nothing more beautiful or precious. Two-eyes saw that the tree had grown up out of the heart of the goat, for it was standing on the exact place where she had buried it. Then the mother said to One-eye, "Climb up, my child, and gather some of the fruit for us."

One-eye climbed up, but when she was about to pick one of the golden apples, the branch eluded her hands, and that happened each time. She could not pick a single apple, however hard she tried. Then the mother said, "Three-eyes, you climb up; you with your three eyes can look about you better than One-eye."

One-eye slid down, and Three-eyes climbed up, but she could not pick the golden apples either. At length the mother grew impatient, and climbed up herself, but did no better than One-eye and Three-eyes, for she always clutched empty air instead of fruit.

Then Two-eyes said, "I'll go up; perhaps I may do better."

The sisters cried, "You indeed, with your two eyes, what can you do?"

But Two-eyes climbed up, and the golden apples did not get out of her way but came into her hand of their own accord, so that she could pick them one after the other, and brought a whole apronful

225

down with her. The mother took them away from her, and instead of treating poor Two-eyes any better for this, she and One-eye and Three-eyes were only envious, and treated her still more cruelly.

It so befell that once when they were all standing together by the tree, a young knight came up.

"Quick, Two-eyes," cried the two sisters, "creep under this, and don't disgrace us!" With all speed they turned an empty barrel over poor Two-eyes, and pushed the golden apples which she had been gathering under it too. The knight was a handsome lord who stopped and admired the magnificent gold and silver tree, and said to the two sisters, "To whom does this fine tree belong? Anyone who gave me one branch might in return ask whatsoever he desired."

Then One-eye and Three-eyes replied that the tree belonged to them, and that they would give him a branch. They both tried hard, but they failed, for the branches and fruit both moved away from them every time. Then said the knight, "It's very strange if the tree belongs to you that you should not be able to break a piece off." They again asserted that the tree was their property.

While they were saying so, Two-eyes rolled out a couple of golden apples from under the barrel to the feet of the knight, for she was vexed with One-eye and Three-eyes for not speaking the truth. When the knight saw the apples he was astonished, and asked where they came from. One-eye and Three-eyes answered that they had another sister, who was not allowed to show herself, for she had only two eyes like any common person. The knight, however, wanted to see her, and cried, "Two-eyes, come forth."

Then Two-eyes came from beneath the barrel, and the knight was surprised at her great beauty, and said, "I'm sure that you can break a branch from the tree for me."

"Yes," replied Two-eyes, "that I certainly can do, for the tree belongs to me."

And she climbed up, and with the greatest ease broke off a branch with beautiful silver leaves and golden fruit, and gave it to the knight.

Then the knight said, "Two-eyes, what shall I give you for it?"

"Alas!" answered Two-eyes. "I suffer from hunger and thirst, grief and want, from early morning till late night; if you would take me with you and deliver me from these things, I should be happy."

So the knight lifted Two-eyes on to his horse, and took her home with him to his father's castle, and there he gave her beautiful clothes, and meat and drink to her heart's content; and as he loved her so much he married her, and the wedding was solemnized with great rejoicing.

Two-eyes' two sisters bitterly grudged her her good fortune. "The wonderful tree, however, still remains with us," thought they, "and even if we can't gather fruit from it, still everyone will come to us and admire it. Who knows what good things may be in store for us?" But next morning, the tree had vanished, and all their hopes were at an end. And when Two-eyes looked out of the window of her own room in the castle, to her great delight it was standing in front of it. It had followed her!

Two-eyes lived a long and happy life. Once two poor women came to her castle, and begged for alms. She looked in their faces and recognized her sisters, One-eye and Three-eyes, who were now so poor that they had to wander about and beg bread from door to door. Two-eyes, however, made them both welcome, and was kind to them, so that they both with all their hearts repented the evil that they had done their sister in their youth.

The Fox
and the Horse

A peasant once had a faithful horse, but he had grown old and could do no more work, so his master grudged him his food and said, "I can get no more work from you, but I mean well by you; if you prove yourself strong enough to bring me a lion, I'll keep you. But now take yourself away out of my stable." And with that he chased him into the open country.

The horse was sad, and went to the forest to shelter from the weather. A fox met him and said, "Why do you hang your head, and go about all alone?"

"Alas," replied the horse, "avarice and fidelity cannot dwell together. My master has forgotten my long service to him, and because I can no longer plough well, he will give me no more food, and has driven me out."

"Without giving you a chance?" asked the fox.

"The chance was a poor one. He said, if I were still strong enough to bring him a lion, he would keep me, but he well knows that I cannot do that."

"I will help you," said the fox. "Just stretch yourself out as if you were dead, and do not stir."

The horse did as the fox desired, and the fox went to the lion, who

228

had his den not far off, and said, "A dead horse is lying outside there. Just come with me; you can have a rich meal."

The lion went with him, and when they were both standing by the horse the fox said, "You can't eat in comfort here. I tell you what: I'll fasten the horse to you by the tail, and then you can drag it into your cave and devour it in peace."

This plan pleased the lion. He lay down while the fox tied the horse fast to him. But the fox tied the lion's legs together with the horse's tail, and twisted and knotted it so well that nothing could undo it. When he had finished, he tapped the horse on the shoulder and said, "Pull, old grey, pull!"

Then up sprang the horse at once, and dragged the lion away behind him. The lion began to roar so that all the birds in the forest flew out in terror, but the horse let him roar, and galloped off until he reached his master's door. When the master saw the lion, he was delighted, and said to the horse, "You can stay with me, and I'll treat you well." And he gave the horse plenty to eat as long as he lived.

Master Pfriem

Master Pfriem was a short, thin, lively man, never still a moment. He had a turned-up nose, his hair was grey and shaggy, his eyes small, glancing perpetually on all sides. He saw everything, criticized everything, and was always in the right.

By trade he was a shoemaker, and when he worked he pulled his thread out with such force that he hit everyone near him. No apprentice stayed more than a month with him, for he had always some fault to find with the very best work: the stitches were not even, one shoe was too long, or one heel higher than the other, or the leather not cut large enough.

"Wait," said he to his apprentice. "I'll soon show you how to make skins soft," and he brought a strap and gave him a couple of strokes across the back. He called them all sluggards. He himself did not get much work done for he never sat still for a quarter of an hour. If his wife got up very early in the morning and lighted the fire, he jumped out of bed, and ran bare-footed into the kitchen, crying, "You'll burn my house down! That's a fire one could roast an ox by! Does wood cost nothing?" If the servants were standing by their wash-tubs and laughing, he scolded them, and said, "There stand the geese cackling, gossiping instead of working. And why fresh soap? Disgraceful extravagance and shameful idleness into the bargain! They want to

231

save their hands, and not rub the things properly!" And out he would run and knock a pail full of soap and water over, so that the whole kitchen was flooded.

Someone was building a new house, so he hurried to the window to look on.

"There, they are using that red sandstone again that never dries!" cried he. "No one will ever be healthy in that house! And just look how badly the fellows are laying the stones! Besides, the mortar is good for nothing! It ought to have gravel in it, not sand. I shall live to see that house tumble down on the people who are in it." He sat down, put a couple of stitches in, and then jumped up again, unfastened his leather apron, and cried, "I'll just go out, and appeal to those men's consciences." He stumbled on the carpenters. "What's this?" cried he, "You are not working with a line! Do you expect the beams to be straight? One wrong will put it all wrong."

Pfriem in a rage ran back into his workshop. When he was setting to work again, the apprentice handed him a shoe.

"Haven't I told you you ought not to cut shoes so broad?" screamed the shoemaker. "Who would buy a shoe like this, which is hardly anything else but a sole? I insist on my orders being followed exactly."

"Master," answered the apprentice, "the shoe may be a bad one, but it is the one which you yourself cut out. When you jumped up a while since, you knocked it off the table, and I have merely picked it up."

One night Master Pfriem dreamed he was dead, and on his way to heaven. When he got there, he knocked loudly at the door. "I wonder," said he to himself, "that they have no knocker on the door – one knocks one's knuckles sore." St Peter opened the door.

"Ah, it's you, Master Pfriem," said he. "Well, I'll let you in, but I warn you that you must give up that habit of yours, and find fault with nothing you see in heaven, or you may fare ill."

"I don't need your warning," answered Pfriem. "I know already what is seemly, and here, God be thanked, everything is perfect, and there is nothing faulty as there is on earth."

He went in, and walked up and down the wide expanses of heaven. He looked around him, to the left and to the right, but sometimes shook his head, or muttered something to himself. Then he saw two angels who were carrying away a beam. It was the beam which someone had had in his own eye while he was looking for the splinter in the eye of another. They did not, however, carry the beam lengthways, but slanting.

"Did anyone ever see such a piece of stupidity?" thought Master Pfriem; but he said nothing. "It comes to the same thing after all, whichever way they carry the beam, straight or crooked, if they only get on with it, and in fact I don't see them knocking against anything."

Soon after this he saw two angels drawing water out of a well into a bucket, but the bucket was full of holes, and the water was running out of it on every side. They were watering the earth with rain. "Hang it," he exclaimed; but happily recollected himself. He went further and saw a cart stuck fast in a deep hole. "It's no wonder," said he to the man who stood by it. "You have loaded it very badly. What is in it?"

"Good wishes," replied the man. "I have pushed it safely so far, and they won't leave me sticking here." In fact an angel came and harnessed two horses to it. "Two horses won't get that cart out," thought Pfriem; "it needs at least four." Another angel came and brought two more horses; she did not, however, harness them in front of it, but behind. That was too much for Master Pfriem.

"Stupid creature," he burst out, "what are you doing? Has anyone since the world began seen a cart drawn in that way? But you, in your arrogance, think that you know everything best."

He was going to say more, but one of the inhabitants of heaven seized him by the throat and pushed him out. Beneath the gateway Master Pfriem turned his head round to take one more look at the cart, and saw that it was being raised into the air by four winged horses.

At this moment, Master Pfriem awoke. "Things are certainly done differently in heaven," said he to himself, "and that excuses much; but who can see horses harnessed both behind and before without protesting? To be sure they had wings, but who could know that? Besides, it's great folly to fix a pair of wings to a horse that has four legs to run with already! But I must get up, or else nothing will go right in the house. It's lucky for me, though, that I'm not really dead."

A Sad Story about a Snake

There was once a child whose mother gave her every afternoon a small bowl of bread and milk, and the child would eat it in the yard. One day, when she began to eat, a snake came creeping out of a crevice in the wall, dipped its head in the dish, and ate with her. This delighted the child. After that, if the snake did not come at once, she cried,

> *"Snake, snake, swiftly come,*
> *Hither come, you little thing.*
> *You shall have some crumbs of bread.*
> *You shall feed yourself with milk."*

Then the snake came and enjoyed its food. In gratitude it brought the child all kinds of pretty things from its hidden treasures: bright stones, pearls, and golden toys. The snake, however, only drank the milk, and left the breadcrumbs.

One day the child took her spoon and tapped the snake gently on its head with it, and said, "Eat the breadcrumbs as well, little thing."

Her mother, who was standing in the kitchen, heard the child talking to someone, and when she saw her, as she thought, striking a snake with her spoon, ran out with a log of wood and killed it.

From that time forth, a change came over the child. As long as the snake had eaten with her, she had grown tall and strong, but now she

235

lost her pretty rosy cheeks and wasted away. It was not long before the owls began to cry in the night, and the redbreast to collect branches and leaves for a funeral garland, and soon afterwards the child lay dead.

Snow-white
and the
Seven Dwarfs

Once upon a time in the middle of winter, when the flakes of snow were falling like feathers from the sky, a queen sat sewing at a window framed in black ebony. And while she was sewing and looking out of the window at the snow, she pricked her finger with the needle, and three drops of blood fell upon the snow. The red looked pretty upon the white snow, and she thought to herself, "If only I had a child as white as snow, as red as blood, and as black as the wood of the window-frame."

Soon after that she had a little daughter, whose skin was white as snow, her cheeks as red as blood, and her hair as black as ebony. They called her Snow-white. But when the child was born, the Queen died.

After a year had passed the King took another wife. She was a beautiful woman, but proud and haughty, and she could not bear that anyone else should surpass her in beauty. She had a magic mirror, and when she looked at herself in it, and said,

> *"Mirror, Mirror, on the wall,*
> *Who is the fairest one of all?"*

the mirror answered,

> *"You, Queen, are the fairest one of all!"*

237

Then she was satisfied, for she knew that the mirror spoke the truth.

Snow-white grew more and more beautiful; and when she was seven years old she was as beautiful as the day, and more beautiful than the Queen herself. One day when the Queen asked her mirror,

> "Mirror, Mirror, on the wall,
> Who is the fairest one of all?"

it answered,

> "You, Queen, both fair and beautous are,
> But Snow-white is lovelier by far."

Then the Queen turned green with envy. From that hour, whenever she looked at Snow-white, her heart pounded – she hated the girl so much.

Envy and pride grew in her heart like a weed, so that she had no peace day or night. She called a huntsman and said, "Take the child into the forest. Kill her, and bring me back her heart as a token." The huntsman took Snow-white away; but when he had drawn his knife to kill her, she began to weep, and said, "Kind huntsman, spare my life! I will run into the wild forest, and never come home again."

And as she was so beautiful the huntsman had pity on her and said, "Run, then, you poor child." "The wild beasts will soon devour her," he thought, and yet it seemed as if a stone had been rolled from his heart since he had not been obliged to kill her. A young boar just then came running by. He stabbed it, and cut out its heart and took it to the Queen. The Queen ordered the cook to serve it up in pickle, and then she ate it, thinking it was Snow-white's heart.

But now poor Snow-white was all alone in the great forest, and so terrified that she did not know what to do. She began to run over sharp stones and through thorns. Wild beasts ran past her, but did her no harm.

She ran until it was almost evening; then she saw a little cottage and went into it to rest. Everything in the cottage was small, but as neat and clean as could be. There was a table with a white cloth and seven little plates, and by each there was a little spoon, a knife and fork, and

a mug. Against the wall stood seven little beds side by side, covered with white counterpanes.

Snow-white was so hungry and thirsty that she ate some vegetables and bread from each plate and drank a drop of wine out of each mug, for she did not wish to take all from one only. Then, as she was so tired, she lay down on one of the little beds, but none of them suited her: one was too long, another too short, but the seventh was just right, so she remained in it, said her prayers and went to sleep.

When it was quite dark the owners of the cottage came back. They were seven dwarfs who dug in the mountains for ore. They lit their seven candles, and by their light saw that someone had been there, for nothing was as they had left it.

The first said, "Who has been sitting on my chair?"

The second, "Who has been eating off my plate?"

The third, "Who has been nibbling my bread?"

The fourth, "Who has been eating my vegetables?"

The fifth, "Who has been using my fork?"

The sixth, "Who has been cutting with my knife?"

The seventh, "Who has been drinking out of my mug?"

Then the first looked and saw that there was a little hollow on his bed, and he said, "Who has been lying on my bed?" The others came up and each called out, "Somebody has been lying on my bed too." But the seventh when he looked at his bed saw Snow-white lying asleep. He called the others, who came running up, and cried out with astonishment, as the light of their candles fell on Snow-white.

"Heavens!" they cried. "What a lovely child!" and they were so delighted that they let her sleep on in the bed. And the seventh dwarf slept with his companions, one hour with each, all through the night.

In the morning Snow-white awoke, and was frightened when she saw the seven dwarfs. But they were friendly and asked what her name was.

"My name is Snow-white," she said.

"What brought you to our house?" asked the dwarfs.

Then she told them how her stepmother had wished to have her killed, how the huntsman had spared her life, and how she had run all day until at last she had found their dwelling. The dwarfs said, "If you will take care of our house, cook, make the beds, wash, sew, and knit, and keep everything neat and clean, you can stay with us and want for nothing."

"Yes," said Snow-white, "with all my heart," and she stayed with them. She kept the house in order for them. In the mornings they went to the mountains and looked for copper and gold, in the evenings they came back, and then their supper had to be ready. The girl was alone the whole day, so the good dwarfs warned her and said, "Beware of your stepmother; she will soon know that you are here; be sure to let no one come in."

But the Queen, believing that she had killed Snow-white, was sure that she was again the fairest of all; and she went to her mirror and said,

> *"Mirror, Mirror, on the wall,*
> *Who is the fairest one of all?"*

and the mirror answered,

> "You, Queen, are fairest in all this land,
> But over the hills, in the greenwood shade,
> Where the seven dwarfs their home have made,
> Snow-white is safely hidden, and she
> Is fairer far, O Queen, to see."

She was dismayed, for she knew that the mirror never lied. She knew too that the huntsman had deceived her, and that Snow-white was still alive. She thought and thought how she might kill her, for so long as she was not the fairest in the whole land, envy let her have no rest. At last she thought of a plan. She stained her face, and dressed herself like an old pedlar-woman, and no one could have known her. In this disguise she went over seven mountains to the home of the seven dwarfs, and knocked at the door and cried, "Pretty things to sell, very cheap, very cheap."

Snow-white looked out of the window and called out, "Good-day, my good woman, what have you to sell?"

"Good things, pretty things," she answered; "stay-laces of all colours," and she pulled out one which was woven of bright coloured silk.

"I'll let the honest old woman in," thought Snow-white, and she unbolted the door and bought the pretty laces.

"Child," said the old woman, "what a fright you look; come, I will lace you properly for once."

Snow-white had no suspicion, but stood before her, and let herself be laced with the new laces. But the old woman laced so quickly and laced so tightly that Snow-white could not breathe and fell down as if dead.

"Now I am the fairest one of all," said the Queen to herself, and hurried away.

Not long after, the seven dwarfs came home, but how shocked they were when they saw their dear Snow-white lying on the ground, without stirring, like one dead. They lifted her up, and when they saw that she was laced too tightly, they cut the laces. At once she began to breathe and soon came to life again. When the dwarfs heard what had

241

happened they said, "The old pedlar-woman was no other than the wicked Queen; take care and let no one come in when we are not here."

But the wicked Queen when she had reached home went in front of the mirror and asked,

> "Mirror, Mirror, on the wall,
> Who is the fairest one of all?"

and it answered as before,

> "You, Queen are fairest in all this land,
> But over the hills, in the greenwood shade,
> Where the seven dwarfs their home have made,
> Snow-white is safely hidden, and she
> Is fairer far, O Queen, to see."

When she heard that, all her blood rushed to her heart with fury for she knew that Snow-white was alive again. "Now," she said, "I must think of something to put an end to her."

With the help of witchcraft, in which she was skilled, she made a poisonous comb. Then she disguised herself and took the shape of another old woman. She went over the seven mountains to the home of the seven dwarfs, knocked at the door, and cried, "Good things to sell, cheap, cheap!"

Snow-white looked out and said, "Go away; I cannot let anyone in."

"At least you can look," said the old woman, and held up the poisonous comb.

Snow-white was so pleased with it that she let herself be beguiled, and opened the door. When they had made a bargain the old woman said, "Now I will comb you properly for once." Poor Snow-white had no suspicion, but hardly had the old woman put the comb in her hair than the poison in it took effect, and the girl fell down senseless.

"You paragon of beauty," said the wicked woman, "you are done for now," and she went away.

Fortunately it was almost evening, when the seven dwarfs came home. When they saw Snow-white lying as if dead upon the ground they at once suspected the stepmother, and they looked and found the poisoned comb. Scarcely had they taken it out when Snow-white came to herself, and told them what had happened. Then they warned her once more to be upon her guard and to open the door to no one.

The Queen, at home, stood in front of the mirror and said,

"Mirror, Mirror, on the wall,
Who is the fairest one of all?"

and it answered as before,

"You, Queen, are fairest in all this land,
But over the hills, in the greenwood shade,
Where the seven dwarfs their home have made,
Snow-white is safely hidden, and she
Is fairer far, O Queen, to see."

When she heard the mirror speak thus she trembled with rage. "Snow-white shall die," she cried, "even if it costs me my life!"

She went into a secret room, and made a poisonous apple. Outside it looked very pretty: red on one side, yellow on the other, so that everyone who saw it longed for it; but whoever ate it must surely die.

When the apple was ready she stained her face, dressed herself up as a country-woman, and went over the seven mountains to the seven dwarfs. She knocked at the door. Snow-white put her head out of the window and said, "I cannot let anyone in; the seven dwarfs have forbidden me."

"It's all the same to me," answered the woman. "I shall soon get rid of my apples. There, I'll give you one."

"No," said Snow-white, "I dare not take anything."

"Are you afraid of poison?" said the old woman. "Look, I'll cut the apple in two pieces; you eat the red side, and I'll eat the yellow."

The apple was so cunningly made that only the red side was poisoned. Snow-white longed for it, and when she saw that the woman ate part of it she could resist no longer, stretched out her hand and took the poisonous half. Hardly had she bitten into it than she fell down dead.

The Queen looked at her with an evil look, laughed aloud and said, "White as snow, red as blood, black as ebony! This time the dwarfs cannot wake you up again."

And when she asked of the mirror at home,

> *"Mirror, Mirror, on the wall,*
> *Who is the fairest one of all?"*

it answered at last,

> *"You, Queen, are the fairest one of all."*

Then her jealous heart was at rest, so far as a jealous heart can ever be at rest.

When the dwarfs came home in the evening, they found Snow-white lying upon the ground dead. They lifted her up, looked to see whether they could find anything poisonous, unlaced her, combed her hair, washed her with water and wine, but it was all no use: the poor child was dead, and remained dead. They laid her upon a bier, and all seven of them sat round it and wept for her three days long.

They were going to bury her, but she still looked as if she were living, and still had her pretty red cheeks. They said, "We can't bury her in the dark ground," and they made a transparent glass coffin, so that she could be seen from all sides, and they laid her in it, and wrote her name upon it in golden letters, and that she was a King's daughter. Then they put the coffin out upon the mountain, and one of them always stayed by it and watched it. And birds came too, and mourned for Snow-white: first an owl, then a raven, and last a dove.

Now Snow-white lay a long, long time in the coffin, looking as if she were asleep. One day a prince came into the forest, and went to the dwarfs' house to spend the night. He saw the coffin on the mountain, and beautiful Snow-white in it, and read what was written upon it in gold letters. Then he said to the dwarfs, "Let me have the coffin. I will give you whatever you want for it."

But the dwarfs answered, "We will not part with it for all the gold in the world."

"Then let me have it as a gift," he said, "for I cannot live without seeing Snow-white. I will honour and prize her as my dearest possession." He spoke so movingly that the good dwarfs took pity upon him, and gave him the coffin.

The prince had it carried away by his servants on their shoulders.

Now it happened that they stumbled over a tree-stump, and with the jolt the poisonous piece of apple which Snow-white had bitten off came out of her throat. Before long she opened her eyes, lifted up the lid of the coffin, sat up, and was once more alive.

"Oh, heavens, where am I?" she cried.

The prince, full of joy, said, "You are with me," and told her what had happened. "I love you more than anything in the world," he said. "Come with me to my father's palace and be my wife."

Snow-white was willing, and went with him, and their wedding was celebrated with great splendour. But Snow-white's wicked step-mother was invited to the feast. When she had put on her beautiful clothes she stood before the mirror, and said,

> "Mirror, Mirror, on the wall,
> Who is the fairest one of all?"

and the mirror answered,

> "You, lady, are fairest here, I ween,
> But fairer far is the new made Queen."

Then the wicked woman uttered a curse, and was so utterly wretched that she didn't know what to do. She had no peace, but felt she must go to see the young Queen. And when she recognized Snow-white she stood rooted to the spot with rage and fear. But iron slippers had already been put upon the fire, and they were brought in with tongs, and set before her. Then she was forced to put on the red-hot shoes, and dance until she dropped down dead.

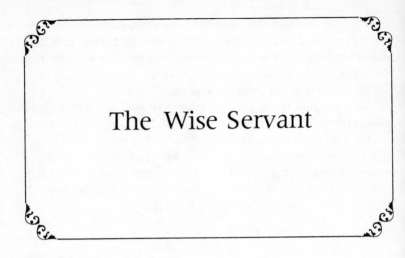

The Wise Servant

How fortunate is the master who has a wise servant who listens to his orders and does not obey them, but prefers to follow his own wisdom. John, a clever servant, was once sent by his master to seek a lost cow. He stayed away a long time, and the master thought, "Faithful John does not spare any pains over his work!" As, however, he did not come back at all, the master was afraid lest some misfortune had befallen him, and set out himself to look for him. He had to search a long time, but at last he saw the boy running up and down a large field.

"Now, John," said the master, "have you found the cow?"

"No, master," he answered, "I haven't found the cow, but then I haven't looked for it."

"Then what have you been looking for, John?"

"Something better, and luckily I have found it."

"What's that, John?"

"Three blackbirds," answered the boy.

"And where are they?" asked the master.

"I see one of them, I hear the other, and I'm running after the third," answered the wise boy.

Take example by this. Do not trouble yourselves about your masters or their orders, but rather do what comes into your head and pleases you, and then you will act just as wisely as prudent John.

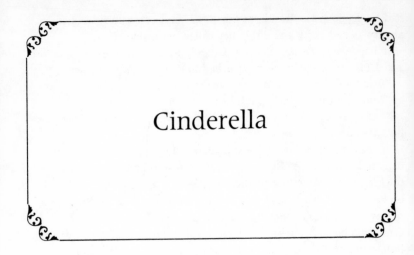

Cinderella

The wife of a rich man fell sick, and as she felt that her end was drawing near, she called her only daughter to her bedside and said, "Dear child, be good and pious, and then God will always protect you, and I will look down on you from heaven and be near you." Then she closed her eyes and died. Every day the maiden went out to her mother's grave and wept, and she remained pious and good. When winter came the snow spread a white sheet over the grave, and when the spring sun had drawn it off again, the man had taken another wife.

The woman brought two daughters into the house with her, who were beautiful and fair of face, but vile and black of heart. Now began a sad time for the poor stepchild.

"Is this stupid goose to sit in the parlour with us?" said they. "Whoever wants to eat bread must earn it. Go and sit with the kitchen-wench." They took her pretty clothes away from her, put an old grey gown on her, and gave her wooden shoes. "Just look at the proud princess, decked out in finery!" they laughed, and led her into the kitchen. There she had to do hard work from morning till night, get up before daybreak, carry water, light fires, cook and wash. Besides this, the sisters mocked her and emptied her peas and lentils into the ashes, so that she was forced to sit and pick them out again. In the evening when she had worked till she was weary she had no bed to go to, but had to sleep by the fireside in the ashes. And as on that account she always looked dusty and dirty, they called her Cinderella.

It happened one day that the father was going to the fair, and he asked his two stepdaughters what he should bring back for them.

"Beautiful dresses," said one. "Pearls and jewels," said the second.

"And you, Cinderella," said he, "what will you have?"

"Father, break off for me the first branch which knocks against your hat on your way home."

So he bought beautiful dresses, pearls and jewels for his two step-daughters, and on his way home, as he was riding through a green thicket, a hazel-twig brushed against him and knocked off his hat. He broke off the branch and took it with him. When he reached home he gave his stepdaughters the things which they had wished for, and to Cinderella he gave the branch from the hazel-bush. Cinderella thanked him, went to her mother's grave and planted the branch on it, and wept so much that the tears fell down on it and watered it. It took root and became a handsome tree. Three times a day Cinderella went and sat beneath it, and wept and prayed, and a little white bird always perched on the tree, and if Cinderella expressed a wish, the bird threw down to her what she had wished for.

Now it happened that the King appointed a festival which was to last three days, to which all the beautiful young girls in the country were invited, in order that his son might choose himself a bride. When the two stepsisters heard that they too were to be present, they were delighted, called Cinderella and said, "Comb our hair for us, brush our shoes and fasten our buckles, for we are going to the festival at the King's palace."

Cinderella obeyed, but wept, because she too would have liked to go to the festival, and begged her stepmother to allow her to do so.

"You go, Cinderella!" she said. "You are dusty and dirty, and you have no clothes and shoes, and yet you want to go to the festival!"

As, however, Cinderells went on asking, the stepmother at last said, "I have thrown a dish of lentils into the ashes. If you have picked them out again in two hours, you shall go with us."

The maiden went into the garden, and called, "Pigeons, turtle-doves, and all you birds of the air, come and help me,

> *The good into the pot throw.*
> *The bad into your crops shall go."*

Then two white pigeons came in by the kitchen window, and the turtle-doves, and at last all the birds of the air flocked in and alighted among the ashes. And the pigeons nodded with their heads and began pick, pick, pick, pick, and the rest began also, pick, pick, pick, pick, and gathered all the good grains into the dish. After barely an hour they had finished, and flown out again. Then the girl took the dish to her stepmother, happy that now she would be allowed to go and dance.

But her stepmother said, "It's no good – you can't come with us. You have no clothes and you cannot dance. We should be ashamed of you!" She turned her back on Cinderella, and hurried away with her two proud daughters.

As no one was now at home, Cinderella went to her mother's grave beneath the hazel-tree, and cried,

> *"Shiver and quiver, little tree,*
> *Silver and gold throw over me."*

Then the little white bird threw a gold and silver dress down to her, and slippers embroidered with silk and silver. She put on the dress with all speed, and went to the dance. Her stepsisters and stepmother however did not know her, and thought she must be a foreign princess, for she looked so beautiful. The prince went to meet Cinderella, took her by the hand and danced with her. He would dance with no other maiden, and if anyone else came to invite her, he said, "She is my partner."

She danced till it was night, and then she wanted to go home. But the prince said, "I will go with you," for he wanted to see where she lived. She escaped from him, however, and sprang into the pigeon-cote. The prince waited until her father came, and told him that the unknown maiden had leapt into the pigeon-cote. The old man thought, "Can it be Cinderella?" They brought him an axe so that he might hew the pigeon-cote to pieces, but no one was inside it. And when they got home Cinderella lay in her dirty clothes among the ashes. A dim little oil lamp was burning on the mantelpiece. Cinderella had jumped quickly out of the pigeon-cote and run to the little hazel-tree. There she had taken off her beautiful clothes and laid them on the grave, and the bird had taken them away again. Then she had settled herself in the kitchen among the ashes in her old grey gown.

Next day when the festival began afresh, and her parents and the stepsisters had gone once more, Cinderella went to the hazel-tree and said,

> *"Shiver and quiver, little tree,*
> *Silver and gold throw over me."*

Then the bird threw down a much more beautiful dress than on the preceding day. And when Cinderella appeared at the dance in this dress, everyone was astonished at her beauty. The prince had waited until she came, and instantly took her hand and danced with no one but her. When others came and invited her, he said, "She is my partner."

When night came she wanted to leave, and the prince followed her, to see into which house she went. But she sprang away from him, and into the garden behind the house. There stood a beautiful tall tree on which hung the most delicious pears. She climbed as nimbly as a squirrel up into the branches, and the prince did not know where she had gone. He waited until her father came, and said to him, "The unknown maiden has escaped from me, and I think she climbed into the pear-tree." The father thought, "Can it be Cinderella?" and had an axe brought and cut the tree down, but no one was on it. When they got into the kitchen, Cinderella lay there among the ashes as usual, for she had jumped down on the other side of the tree, had taken the beautiful dress to the bird on the little hazel-tree, and put on her old grey gown.

On the third day, when the parents and sisters had gone, Cinderella once more went to her mother's grave and said to the little tree,

> *"Shiver and quiver, little tree,*
> *Silver and gold throw over me."*

Then the bird threw down to her a dress which was more magnificent

251

than any she had yet had. And when she went to the festival everyone was speechless at her beauty. The prince danced only with her, and if anyone invited her to dance, he said, "She is my partner."

When evening came, Cinderella wanted to leave, and the prince was anxious to go with her, but she escaped from him so quickly that he could not follow her. The prince had, however, used a stratagem, and had caused the whole staircase to be smeared with cobbler's wax, so that, when she ran down, the maiden's left slipper remained sticking there. The prince picked it up. It was small and dainty, and all of gold.

Next morning, he went with it to Cinderella's father and said to him, "No one shall be my wife but she whose foot this golden slipper fits." The two sisters were delighted, for they had pretty feet. The eldest took the shoe into her room to try it on, and her mother stood by. But she could not get her big toe into it. The shoe was too small for her. Then her mother handed her a knife and said, "Cut off the toe. When you are Queen you won't need to go on foot."

The maiden cut the toe off, forced the foot into the shoe, endured the pain, and went out to the prince. He took her upon his horse as his bride and rode away with her. However, they had to pass the grave, and there, on the hazel-tree, sat two pigeons who cried,

> "Turn and look, turn and look,
> There's blood within the shoe.
> The shoe is much too small for her.
> The true bride waits for you."

Then he looked at her foot and saw how the blood was streaming from it. He turned his horse round and took the false bride home again, and said she was not the true one, and that the other sister was to put the shoe on. She went into her chamber and got her toes safely into the shoe, but her heel was too large. So her mother handed her a knife and said, "Cut a bit off your heel. When you are Queen you won't need to go on foot."

The maiden cut a bit off her heel, forced her foot into the shoe, endured the pain, and went out to the prince. He took her upon his horse as his bride, and rode away with her, but when they passed by the hazel-tree, the two pigeons sat on it and cried,

"Turn and look, turn and look,
There's blood within the shoe.
The shoe is much too small for her.
The true bride waits for you."

He looked down at her foot and saw how the blood was running out of her shoe. Then he turned his horse and took the false bride home again.

"This is not the right one either," said he. "Have you no other daughter?"

"No," said the man. "There is only a little kitchen-wench which my late wife left behind her, but she cannot possibly be the bride."

The prince said she must be sent for, but the mother answered, "Oh no, she is much too dirty; she mustn't be seen!"

He insisted, and Cinderella had to be called. She first washed her hands and face, then went and curtsied to the prince, who handed her the golden slipper. Then she sat down on a stool, pulled off her heavy wooden clog, and put on the slipper, which fitted like a glove. When she stood up, the prince recognized the beautiful maiden who had danced with him, and cried, "This is the true bride!"

The stepmother and the two sisters turned pale with rage, but he took Cinderella upon his horse and rode away with her.

As they passed by the hazel-tree, the two white pigeons cried,

> "Turn and look, turn and look,
> No blood is in the shoe.
> The shoe is not too small for her.
> The true bride rides with you."

and the two came flying down and perched on Cinderella's shoulders, one on the right, the other on the left, and stayed there till they reached the palace.